SHE] HOLMES

A
Scandalous
Affair

Includes Bonus Story
SHERLOCK HOLMES
The Egyptian Ring

Christopher D. Abbott

Other Titles

MYSTERY

Sir Laurence Dies [The "Dies" Series - Book 1]
Dr. Chandrix Dies [The "Dies" Series - Book 2]
SHERLOCK HOLMES: A Scandalous Affair

FANTASY

Songs of the Osirian [Songs of the Osirian - Book 1]
Rise of the Jackal King [Songs of the Osirian - Book 2]
Daughter of Ra [Songs of the Osirian - Book 3]
Citadel of Ra [Songs of the Osirian - Book 4]
Songs of the Osirian: Companion

SUPERNATURAL/HORROR

Progenitor

ANTHOLOGIES

All That Remains
Beast: A New Beginning
Beast: Revelations

HORROR

Escaping Matilda
Revolting Tales: Christopher D. Abbott & Todd A. Curry

CONTENTS

Other Titles

SHERLOCK HOLMES

A
Scandalous
Affair

Foreword

At the latter end of 1903, Sherlock Holmes retired from consulting practice, choosing to leave the hustle of London life and set up home in a small farm on the Sussex Downs. During these early days, Holmes' only concerns were for his beehives and technical manuals. As time moved on, however, he tired of country life and accepted cases that gave him the mental stimulation he often craved. There were many cases of note, leading right up to the Great War of 1914. On some of those cases, I was fortunate to have played a small role. The sources of late-night stories around a fire, which I wrote as best as I could, being ever eager to add something new to my catalogue. Those I was engaged in, had more detail than those dictated to me. And until his death he remained clear on which cases I could publish, and those the eyes of the public should never see.

Sherlock Holmes undertook cases in the strictest confidence, and not always for financial gain. In fact, often he'd turned down what he referred to as "dull engagements" from wealthy clients, in favour of more interesting challenges from those with no means financially. Holmes investigated each case without prejudice. His professionalism could never be questioned but often was. Money could not sway him, and nor could the idea of fame. It might not be clear, but many of the cases he undertook for official police agencies came with zero credit, recognition, or compensation. I still receive letters of complaint from retired policemen, aggrieved by the audacity of my publishing versions of their cases which detailed Holmes having solved them instead. I saw it as the official record being "set straight", they did not.

I've often remarked Holmes had a singular gift for observation. But as time went on, we met others with equal gifts. Holmes in later years took a few what he called "rough diamonds" and instructed them on the practical application of his craft. Nevertheless, he was the master and to my mind, always will be.

Since Holmes' passing. I have unsealed cases that could have no harmful bearing on any members of the families still related to them. But, in consideration of the instructions my late friend laid out, I consulted and warned all living family members before publishing.

The case I am about to narrate was during a time when Holmes was not in good physical and psychological health. Without a case on hand, he could be destructive to himself, and to his friends. Years later, he would come to recognise and find better ways to stabilise his moods, but in those early years, he would address it either chemically or through mental stimulation. I always hoped for the latter, but he often settled for the former. However, these maladies did not seem to diminish his skills, even with the passing of time. Holmes' mind remained sharp, even as he weakened physically. The mental health of my friend has never been a topic for publishing. But since I have grown older, and wiser on the subject, my writings shall not avoid it entirely.

I've remarked on occasion that Holmes often decried my "romanticisms". He wanted me to write cases more in line with scientific papers. He lamented on how I would degrade a "series of lectures" into "asinine tales for the witless public". He wasn't wrong. He once said something like: 'Your error was in attempting to put colour and soul into your statements, instead of confining yourself to placing on record that severe reasoning from cause to effect, being the only notable feature about the case.' (Forgive me for not fully remembering the exact wording he used). Later in life, Holmes came to recognise the need to add flare and colour. When he attempted to write his own cases up, he found no one wanted to read them as scientific studies of the art of deduction. They wanted a story. He would blame that on me too.

I wrote this story twenty-five years ago to the day. I may have touched up one or two lines but it isn't representative of a man attempting to recall his past. It is the reflection of a man from the summer of 1899.

I had been to Scotland for relaxation and a break from London and–if I'm honest–from Holmes. At that time, he had become almost impossible to live with. Nevertheless, after the fishing became monotonous, and the social scene mundane, I found myself missing what I had come to escape. So, with my bags packed I hurried back home. As it happens at the right time, since the day I arrived coincided with a visit from Inspector Hargreaves of the Kent County Constabulary.

And that's where this story begins. With Inspector Hargreaves attempting to persuade Sherlock Holmes to look into the apparent suicide of Lieutenant James Wilson...

John H. Watson, MD (retd.), 1924

Chapter One

It was late afternoon when we pulled into King's Cross station. After making my way through the ticket office, I found myself outside amongst the hectic streets of London. There was something rather comforting about being back in the "normal" hustle and bustle of a busy city. A far cry from the more subdued countryside I had left the previous night.

London is a hub of activity at most times of the day, and never more so mid-afternoon. Finding a cab could be a real challenge, so it wasn't an unexpected frustration when it took almost thirty minutes to see one. While I waited, I observed children scuttling between couples walking along the station road. The summer air was warm enough, but as the day waned, a cold air crept in with it, attracting many of the city's poor to the warmth of the station. I could see some of them already setting up camps for the cold evening ahead. Police officers fought a losing battle to move several on, and it reminded me of how far we still had to go to change the state of the inequality of our economic system. I had always been of the opinion an extra penny on the income tax could help finance institutions better to serve those who were in need. But that position was not popular with those who could influence such change.

It wasn't long before a Hansom cab stopped to deliver a couple outside the station concourse, and I was able to take it. The driver leant forward, looking down through the opened hatch on top of the carriage.

'Where to, Guv?' he asked politely.

We exchanged details. He then tipped his hat and closed the hatch, and I was finally on my way home.

The route took us past the City and Suburban Bank. I smiled. It recalled to my mind the case where Holmes had helped to save the bank the loss of its recent consignment of French gold. An affair we later discovered perpetrated by agents of the evil and brilliant Professor Moriarty–my friend's nemesis–who thought to end his career, but ultimately ended his own, along with his life.

The cab passed Regent's Park where the night attracted some of the city's criminal elements. I was alert during this phase of my journey. If my time with Holmes had proven anything, it was one could not be too careful on a London street at night. I was therefore relieved when we passed Park Road and turned into Upper Baker Street. A place where those same elements dared never to go.

The journey had taken around forty minutes all-in-all and, weary from my long travels, I disembarked and entered the familiar warmth of my home. I was greeted by Wiggins, our pageboy. Since Holmes' practice had grown, it was not unusual to find Wiggins tending the door. Mrs Hudson lamented the need to be doorkeeper all hours of the day and night, to the many visitors who called, so Holmes employed Wiggins a few days a week to placate her.

When the evening was shut out by the closing of our front door, Wiggins took my cane and hat and dropped them in their customary place. I removed my heavy overcoat and hung it on the coatrack by the door. Wiggins–not the most educated or articulate of lads–explained Mrs Hudson was sick with (in his cockney tongue) "in-flo-em-za". I knew what he meant. It turned out the doctor on call who had taken care of her was a colleague of mine, so I assumed the duties with eagerness.

Mrs Hudson, although told to remain in bed, did nothing of the sort and came to greet me. Wrapped in a heavy grey cardigan, I could tell by her waxing skin and pallor she was not out of her illness's clutches.

'Welcome home, Doctor. How was your trip?'

In a brief exchange, I told her all about it. Actually, I told her what I thought she'd want to hear. No one really needs to know the holiday you had been harping on about for weeks turned out to be mundane. Mrs Hudson nodded with an interest I could tell was polite.

'I expect you'll be wanting your bed soon enough. I have some broth boiling, if you would care to join me?'

I nodded.

She gazed up the stairs. 'I should warn you. Mr Holmes has been in a terrible mood since you left. It has been a long three weeks. I don't mind telling you. Mr Holmes won't eat, won't see anybody, and spends the night pacing up and down his room.' She sighed. 'Twice I have tried to get him to open his door; twice he has sent me away. He is not well, Doctor, not well at all.'

Mrs Hudson was a strong Scottish woman. She had a maternal care for Holmes, but that care had limits. It was obvious hers had been reached.

'It can't go on, Doctor. It really can't.'

'I understand,' I said, trying to sooth her. 'Let me worry about Mr Holmes. You just concentrate on getting better, okay?'

She nodded and offered a faint smile. 'I am glad you're back, Doctor,' she reiterated, 'really I am. But before you go up, let's both have some broth. We could use the strength from it. You'll need it more than I.'

I agreed and followed her into the kitchen. I pet her hand and she seemed to draw strength from it. We talked for a while, each with a bowl of her broth—Mrs Hudson was an exceptional cook—and I was happier knowing that she had eaten.

When we had finished, I left her and mentally prepared myself to attend Holmes. As I started up the stairs, I heard Mrs Hudson shuffle off towards her rooms. And then she called out to me, drawing from her pocket a collection of telegrams.

'I tried to give these to him. He wouldn't open the door. I could have poked them under, but I can't be bending down at my age.'

Mrs Hudson handed them over.

'I'll give them to him.'

From a brief examination of the sender information, they'd come from an Inspector Hargreaves of Dartford Police Station, in the Kent Constabulary. I was very fond of Dartford town, and it had been several years since I had been.

I made my way up the stairs to our landing. On reaching the rooms I shared with my friend, I found them locked.

I knocked.

'Go away, Mrs Hudson!' came an abrupt reply.

I took in a breath. 'Holmes, it's Watson. Open the door … there's a good chap.' I heard a commotion from within. It sounded like a table falling over and our hat stand along with it. After a lot of cursing and rummaging, the lock clicked, and the door swung inwards. I peered in to see the devastation I expected. I was aghast.

I had correctly surmised a table with its contents knocked over. Holmes' files, which he usually kept in strict order, were now spread transversely across the floor beside his chair.

And standing amidst it all was Sherlock Holmes.

'It's about time you came back.'

As expected, Holmes was in a foul mood. But that bothered me less than the nervous agitation he exhibited. It was far worse than I envisaged.

'How am I to tend to the latest unrecorded incidences of lost pets if my chief biographer is running around the depths of the Hampshire dales?' He wore the mouse-coloured dressing gown, along with a look of desperation on his pale angular face. His features were gaunt and his lean frame thinner. His eyes bulged from their sockets. In all our time together, he had never looked so ill.

I put on a smile. 'It's good to see you too, Holmes.'

I attempted to mentally prepare myself for the difficult task ahead. He gestured me in with a wave and made off in an energetic dash towards his bedroom.

'How was Hampshire anyway?' he shouted.

I picked up the table and the contents. 'Scotland, Holmes, as you well know. And it was fine, for a time. The weather was good. The fishing was better.' I continued around the room, returning strewn items to their original place. 'I met some interesting people, but after a while, I began to miss...' I looked around me and sighed. 'This.'

I observed his rapid washing, and wondered how long it had been since he'd done so, and how long that water had sat there. Not being one to hold back in matters of health, I commented on his.

'You're more agitated than usual.' I reached for my medical bag and looked up when I heard movement beside me.

'You can put that down,' he hissed. 'There's nothing you could possess in there that could help me.' He stepped up to the window and stared outside.

'I'm at the end, dear Watson. Drawn to the precipice. I have not had a case now for over three weeks and I fear if I did get one, I'd probably not know how to employ my skills to solve it.' With a huff he returned to his favourite sitting chair and fell in. He then pulled a box from under a growing pile of newspapers, handing it to me.

'You see, I was mindful of your return.' Holmes attempted a smile, but he read the concern from me and looked away. From the way his veins pulsated on his neck and forehead, I knew his heart rate was high. This, amongst other symptoms, solidified my diagnosis of his hypertensive state. His usual go to, should a case not present itself, would be to turn to cocaine, or morphine, or worse. But it appeared this time he had abstained. It relieved me. My warning on the subject, heard. A subject we tried mostly to avoid. Recognising I was unable to assist my friend medically, I sat and lit a cigar, exhaling into the already thick atmosphere of the room.

Perhaps it was my return, or just having another to speak with. Whatever the reason, Holmes seemed to settle. He reached for a long-stemmed pipe and I inwardly smiled. At least he hadn't chosen the clay pipe. That one always matched his disputatious mood. It appeared even Sherlock Holmes was a creature of habit.

Since the death of Professor Moriarty, the instigator of many of the unsolved and undetected crimes in Europe, Holmes had suggested there were no longer any enterprising criminals left. That he, in his arrogance, had removed one-by-one the intellectuals of crime. He often cursed the criminal fraternity for no longer posing any challenge. A thing he desired the most. It was only when in this mood he considered the possibility he had made an error in taking the man down.

When he first spoke of Professor Moriarty, he called him "the Napoleon of crime". In some respects, he was the polar opposite of my friend. Moriarty used his highly developed cognitive abilities to control a vast criminal agency. I think even Holmes recognised London, and maybe Europe, was safer now this Napoleon was gone. Still, I could not help but sympathise, even if my friend's motives were purely selfish. Holmes wanted cases that were a challenge, to meet his great intellect. And the longer he went without them, the worst his depression grew. I was not always successful in helping him change his poor behaviours, but the worst of them, his substance abuse, I could claim victory for. As a medical man, it was difficult to sit back and watch anyone slowly destroy the gifts they relied on. Sadly, it is not possible to persuade someone, however logical your argument might be, when they simply don't want to hear it.

'Did you try the relaxants I prescribed?'

Holmes flashed me a dark look while drawing on his pipe.

'If I am to clear myself of the yearning for the seven percent solution of cocaine, then I will do so without further chemical assistance.' He softened his brow. 'I tell you, Watson, I nearly broke our agreement yesterday afternoon.' He sighed. 'I need to work, Watson. I need to stimulate my brain.'

I nodded and changed tactics. 'Mrs Hudson is worried about you.'

He grunted.

'You shouldn't treat her so poorly. She is our landlady.'

He tightened his lips together, but had the good grace to look down.

I looked over a pile of letters scattered on the floor beside my chair. 'I should have thought there was something of interest in these?'

Holmes held out his hand, and I handed them to him. He threw them in the fire.

'Rubbish, Watson, all of them! Lost cats, missing servants, runaway wives. Really?'

I reached into my pocket and pulled out the collection of telegrams Mrs Hudson had handed me.

'What do you have there?' he asked.

'These? Oh, these telegrams are from an Inspector Hargreaves, from Kent Constabulary. Should I burn them?' I made a move towards the fire, but he stopped me. I hoped they might hold the key to a case of interest. Sometimes it was necessary to provoke a response, rather than coerce one.

A little colour returned to Holmes' cheeks as he took the telegrams. He then waved at his collection of indexes in the corner of our sitting room. I smiled. Holmes had an index on every police officer and official. It didn't take long to find the file he wanted.

His irritation hadn't quite ceased. 'Am I to become a lackey for the police now, too?' It sounded as childish as it was, so I ignored it.

I continued my search through the papers in the file and found the one marked "Police Officers - Kent Constabulary". I couldn't find anything on this inspector.

Holmes had now read through the telegrams several times. He looked up. 'There is nothing strange about that,' he remarked. 'The Dartford Police has not long been fully staffed. It is likely this inspector was either recently promoted, or came from another constabulary of which we've had no prior dealings.' He stood and reached for his tobacco in the Persian slipper hanging from the mantle.

'Well,' he huffed, 'I suppose it beats doing nothing at all. I shall write a response, maybe there's something in it.'

The London fog that often covered the tracks of so many vile criminals was lingering low in the street below. I watched as a carriage drawn by two horses pulled up, the Kentish Constabulary coat of arms marked on the door. I smiled. It did not take a detective to realise who our visitor might be.

'Holmes,' I said, 'you won't need to.'

He frowned, then came beside me at the window.

'A Hansom cab,' I said. 'Pulling up outside our door, and at this hour. What can it mean?'

For the first time that evening Holmes' smile was genuine. 'It means, my dear friend, this Inspector Hargreaves has a modicum of intelligence.'

I watched Wiggins fussing with the carriage door. 'How so?'

'Well,' remarked Holmes, his humour unmistakable, 'he came to consult me, didn't he?'

I chuckled. 'Something dire with any luck.'

Holmes played along. 'A good murder, that's just what we need.'

'With an underlying international twist too?'

Holmes opened the window to freshen the stale room air. 'Wouldn't *that* be a nice change?'

We would later come to regret those words.

Chapter Two

I looked at Holmes who was still wearing his pyjamas. 'You might want to change?'

Holmes looked down. 'Yes. Deal with him while I dress.'

I'm not blowing my own trumpet when I say a normal part of our friendship allowed for me to be the voice of reason in most circumstances, and also, the footman in others. It's no secret Holmes' intellect set him apart from most, and whilst I could not be the detective he was, I was able on occasion to shield him from his inanity. I finished a hurried tidy of our sitting room. From his bedroom I heard Holmes cursing. I looked around with a tight smile. Furniture now upright, files were tidied away. It looked almost normal. Almost.

There was a knock at our door. Mrs Hudson, our long-suffering landlady, entered and scanned the room, her hard expression unmistakable.

'There's a gentleman to see Mr Holmes.' I wish she'd let Wiggins take the lead. She really didn't look well.

Her gaze fell on me and she smirked. 'You would make a good housekeeper, Doctor.' Then raising her voice, meant clearly for Holmes, she said, 'Should I show him up, or just leave him in the cold?'

'Show him up,' he called back.

'You're sure? I mean, three times today you've told me to go away.'

There was a dull thud, a curse, then, 'Mrs Hudson!'

She chuckled then directed her conversation to me. 'Inspector Hargreaves is waiting, Doctor. I'll keep him a moment longer, then send him up.' She looked at the pile of papers stacked on the chairs. As she left, she raised her voice. 'Will that give you enough time to find him somewhere to sit, Mr Holmes?'

'Go away!' came the curt reply.

Not long after, Inspector Hargreaves was shown in by Wiggins.

The inspector was a short fellow with a brown suit, matching bowler, and steady gaze. He wore a bushy moustache and a ruddy complexion. He was a lean man in his mid-to-late thirties. He approached me and extended his hand.

'Ah, Doctor Watson, isn't it?'

He had a very pleasant way about him. Affable but firm. He shook my hand as Wiggins closed the door.

'It is so good to meet you in person. I've read almost everything you've written.'

Another thud and harrumph came from the other room. I thanked him, offering him the seat I'd set up next to ours by the fire. He accepted and sat.

'Mr Holmes will be with us shortly. Can I offer some refreshment until then?'

The inspector shook his head.

'No thank you, Doctor. I've telegrammed four times today. I'm sure I can wait a little longer.'

At that point, the door burst open. Holmes entered dressed in his usual black suit and waistcoat, covered by the mouse-coloured dressing gown he often wore when home. He acknowledged the inspector as he reached the mantle and stood with his back turned towards the fire and lit a cigarette.

'Inspector, I apologise, but I have not had a chance to review your telegrams. Please explain what urgency would necessitate the infringement of my Saturday evening,' said Holmes, his brusque statement typical of his openers for officials. The inspector stood and looked directly at Holmes.

'I see that you haven't had a case for some time?' Hargreaves replied.

Holmes raised an eyebrow. 'Explain how you come to *that* erroneous conclusion?'

'By your complexion. It looks like you've not eaten for days. Large volumes of paperwork are left untended and in disarray. Frankly, you look ill. But not by this awful flu that's doing the rounds. I fancy a lack of mental stimulation might be the cause. I daresay I'm wrong on all accounts.' The inspector sat quietly as Holmes contemplated his response. Eventually he smiled. With a quizzical look at me, he inclined his head and dropped into his favourite chair.

'Very good, Inspector. You have my attention. Some of what you say has merit, even truth. But like my dear friend's work, the rest is fiction I'm afraid.'

Holmes' praise often came at the expense of a dig at me.

Inspector Hargreaves did not falter at Homes' withering gaze. My friend knew how intimidating he could be, so I was pleased to see his eyes soften, if only slightly.

'I suppose,' Hargreaves offered to Holmes' raised eyebrow, 'it is the Doctor's writings which make those observations possible. I meant no disrespect.'

I inwardly cursed. Again, Holmes' eyes found mine. I read more than I wanted in them. He then returned his attention to our guest. 'Indeed. I wish I could say I was impressed.'

I didn't think it would be forgotten. The look he threw me was one only those who share a long history can recognise. Still, he seemed more amused than annoyed. Had the inspector not come with the possibility of a case, I imagine he'd be thrown out, and I subjected to abuse I rarely document.

At length he said, 'It seems, Watson, that once again you exaggerate. It might be prudent to vet your documentation more thoroughly before you next write up a case … and now, Inspector, you have my full attention. Tell me why you need my services.'

I was not off the hook then.

'To business. Mr Holmes, the facts are these.' He drew from his pocket a small notebook and read from it.

Holmes sighed. He sat with his eyes closed and feet drawn up to his chest, hands clasped around his knees. The exchange between the two of them only lasted a few seconds, but I have to say Inspector Hargreaves impressed me.

Holmes' face flushed with colour.

'At eight o'clock this morning, I called upon Reardon house, which is a large residence owned by Sir Henry Wilburton. Although a junior member of government, he has connections across the entire county. His house is in Dartford, Kent. When I arrived, I was taken to the body of a young Lieutenant James Wilson. He'd been found dead in the garden. Wilson was slumped backwards over a bench, the back of his head open. A clear shot visible on his face. There was a revolver still clasped in his left hand. One round fired. According to the police doctor, he'd been there approximately an hour, putting his time of death around seven.'

Holmes put out his cigarette. 'Very concise. Who found the body?'

'That's an interesting question. Several people are claiming to have found him.'

'Very curious. Who called the police?'

The inspector studied his notes. 'This may pique your interest. A telegraph was received from Mr James Wilson at seven o'clock, followed by a telephone call from Sir Henry at seven thirty.' The inspector looked over at Holmes expectantly.

Holmes had picked up his pipe and was tapping it against his teeth. After some time, aware the room was silent, he smiled.

'A telegram and a telephone call? That is interesting.'

The inspector stood and flipped open his book. He paced the room as he spoke. Holmes studied him intently. 'I've been unable to confirm where the original message came from. It can't have been the lieutenant, unless the doctor has his time of death wrong?'

'Do you have it?' Holmes asked.

Hargreaves nodded and handed it over.

Holmes read it aloud. 'From Mr J Wilson of Reardon House. A crime is in progress. Come at once.' He turned it over. 'Date and time stamps seem authentic. Very curious. What happened next?'

'My chief inspector believes the deceased wired a telegram and then killed himself.'

'But you are sceptical?'

'Yes.'

'Why?'

'He and Sir Henry are friends. He didn't even listen to my findings. Just told me to wrap it up quickly and move on. I don't know. Something wasn't right. The household reactions were shifty. Domestics were on edge and unhelpful. I can't finger it properly. It's why I came to you.'

'Now you impress me.' Holmes' posture changed. He became erect and alert. Something had caught his attention. I could not think what, but when his eyes sparkled, and that slow smile spread … it was a look I knew well. He held up a hand. 'One moment, Hargreaves.' He pulled out the telegram and studied it with a frown. 'This is curious. The title of Wilson, on the telegram, you see it? "Mr" and not "Lieutenant".'

Hargreaves also frowned. 'You think it significant?'

He nodded. 'And suggestive.'

The inspector shrugged. 'In the balance, the mistake might just be inconsequential. If it came from Wilson, then my experience tells me it was born from a broken mind. And if it came from someone else, it was probably just an error. After all, what is in a title?'

Holmes sat for some time and then looked up and smiled. 'What indeed.'

I could tell he was pondering the question. He exhibited those unconscious tendencies–like circling the tip of his pipe around his jawbone–this he often did when his thoughts were being ordered.

'But what was the purpose for his telegraph? That is the question we should be asking.'

'It's the question I've been asking too, but no one seems to be interested. A crime is in progress, but what crime? Was it to warn us of unrest in the household? Get help from us to avert a public scandal of some kind? I don't know. I want to know. Anyway, approximately thirty minutes later, Sir Henry called the station on his telephone. He said Wilson had killed himself.' Hargreaves leant forward. 'He's a difficult man, Mr Holmes. Very unhelpful. A nasty sort, if you get my meaning? If there was a scandal in the household, and I'm inclined to think there was, it likely died with Wilson. The motive behind the telegram would seem to be the thing we must uncover.'

Holmes' eyes were unfocused. He remained silent for some time, which was not uncommon. Eventually he said, 'There are singular points to this case which interest me.'

I was relieved to hear that.

'The substance of the telegram is, as you say, important. But I'm interested in its detail. I see you don't comprehend; the mistake in the title used for young Wilson is suggestive in itself.' Holmes' brow creased, and he looked off into the distance.

The inspector waited for Holmes to explain, but as I knew better, I broke the silence.

'What have you done since then, Inspector?'

'Well, Doctor, I made a study of the ground, to see if I could come up with anything. I examined the revolver. It had been fired, and there was a spent case in the locking chamber. All the handguns are cleaned and locked away after they're used. That's something the butler was clear to point out. The grass was moist from the morning dew and I noticed two sets of footprints leading towards the bench, but only one leading away. One belonged to the deceased; the other to Sir Henry. The only conclusion I can reach is the victim had been followed. Perhaps he was enjoying the morning air? Maybe contemplating this crime, the telegram mentioned? Someone killed him, Mr Holmes. And that someone could only have been Sir Henry.'

Holmes regarded him. 'How so?'

'His boots match the prints.'

'His boot prints matched?'

Holmes flashed me a look. It wasn't kind.

'No, no, Inspector!' Holmes moved to the window and looked down at the street below. 'Your evidence is circumstantial. How, for example, have you concluded Sir Henry wore them? Could it not have been somebody who merely wanted the police to think Sir Henry murdered Wilson?'

'It's a hunch. I told you, he's a nasty kind. Volatile. If anyone could do it, it would be him. I'll admit I took an instant dislike to him.'

Holmes leant into the window and let out a breath. 'Inspector, you cannot condemn a man based on feelings. If I were to do so, half of the London elite would be swinging from the end of a rope.'

The inspector opened his mouth to respond, but Holmes waved a hand at him. His pipe dangled from his lips. Holmes smoked for a while and then a thought occurred to him. 'Who is your principal witness?'

The inspector flipped through his notes. 'There are many witnesses. Not all of which are reliable, but if I were to pick one, it would be the butler, Edward Stepson.'

I thought the inspector was doing a good job of keeping things ordered. He was concise with his answers. Holmes being a practical person often forgot others were less organised. He could also strike fear into the most solid of characters. Having confronted difficult and dangerous men, his abilities were sometimes masked by a demanding nature. Throughout our consultation, the inspector, it seemed to me, was keen to make a good impression. My friend, however, was not easily impressed and even if he became so, it could be lost in short order. Although he would never admit it, I believe Holmes was a little prejudiced towards policemen. He gave street urchins less cross-examination.

I said, 'Is this Stepson prepared to say Sir Henry murdered the victim?'

The inspector shook his head. 'No. We questioned him, but he wasn't helpful. Shut up like an oyster in fact. No one noticed anything out of the ordinary. No one could have foreseen such a circumstance. They didn't know why Wilson would do it. Couldn't understand how anyone would think Sir Henry involved … an important man, upright citizen. You get the picture.'

Holmes grunted. 'The butler's avowal of loyalty should be taken for what it's worth.'

The inspector smiled and continued. 'Agreed. I put out a local bulletin, but so far no one has offered any new information. Still, Stepson gave us something. He is prepared to say he saw Wilson leave alone for his walk in the garden. He also said Sir Henry went for an uncustomary walk at around the same time. But as both left in opposite directions, he would swear to the fact Sir Henry could not have been in the garden when Wilson died. The chief inspector believes that's an end to it. And unless I find something better, it will be.'

'I see your difficulty. Any other witnesses or persons of interest?'

Hargreaves nodded. 'A Reverend Jeremy Trelean saw Lieutenant Wilson crossing the lawn. He was the second to last person to see him alive.'

Holmes inclined his head. 'Describe this Trelean to me.'

The inspector referred to his notes. 'Reverend Jeremy Trelean. Medium-build. Late forties. Silver swept-back hair. Very stern-looking man. God fearing type, obviously. He's not local, although he's a bit of a mystery. I talked with the head of the local parish, but they didn't know anything about him. He's only been seen in a few places and has given no sermons. He lives on the Reardon estate. All they could tell me was Reverend Trelean was from London. They say he has a somewhat hypnotic effect on his congregation. It was odd they referred to him as the Vicar, and not Reverend, still, I'm not up on church matters.'

Holmes left the comfort of the windowsill and walked around to the mantle. He tapped out and refilled his pipe. In my experience, Holmes made his mind up on events well in advance. He had a wealth of experience and it often made him appear superior in the eyes of the police. And to me.

'Watson, this place is a mess,' he said, tripping over a pile of papers I had dropped behind his chair when the inspector first entered. 'Well, on reflection, Hargreaves, I agree with your evidence, not your hunch. Your evidence points to murder, but none suggesting Sir Henry had a direct hand in it. I do not dismiss your idea, it is not without merit, but stick to the facts, and not hunches. The body was found after the death occurred, we are all agreed on this, yes?' Holmes looked to each of us.

I thought his question was idiotic. From the inspector's facial expression, I think he agreed with me. 'The body could hardly be found *before* the death, Holmes.'

But Holmes just smiled. It was an annoying smile.

'It may seem like a ridiculous assertion, but I assure you, there is a valid reason behind my asking it. Let us change direction. To you, Inspector, I would caution. The footprints you discovered cannot aid you in your quest to find Sir Henry guilty of murder.'

'How so?'

'Your own evidence answers it. I suggest to you Sir Henry found the body, then returned to the house to call the police. Surely *this* is a more reasonable interpretation of the facts?'

'Except he denies having gone near the body.'

'Yes, and half the household are claiming responsibility to shield him. He's a powerful man. I am sure disloyalty is treated harshly in that household.'

Hargreaves frowned. 'I agree, but why would he lie about that? And why would someone lie to cover up his lie?'

Holmes' eyes sparkled. 'Excellent.' He clapped his hands. 'Very good questions, Inspector. But let us move away from that for a moment. There is one other point concerning me. Why a telegram? That is outré and suggestive. I see you both fail to follow my reasoning. It is just possible someone did not know there was a modern telephone in the house, you see where this new data takes us?'

'It suggests an outsider sent a telegram?' the inspector answered.

'Watson?'

I thought about it for a moment. 'Yes, I agree. Someone unfamiliar with the house may have been involved. An outsider, as you say, Inspector? A third person, perhaps.'

Holmes nodded. 'A third person indeed. And then here is my second point of concern. The time needed to organise and send a telegram.'

Hargreaves hit his head. 'My god, that did not occur to me.'

I frowned. 'I am missing this point, sorry.'

The inspector smiled at Holmes. 'It came in at seven. At the time they supposedly found the body.'

I was still confused. 'So?'

Hargreaves ran with it. 'So, it's easily a twenty-five-minute walk to the telegraph office, Doctor. Wilson would have been alive before whoever left to send it.'

Holmes clapped. 'Excellent, Inspector.'

'I need to find out who sent that telegram.'

Holmes nodded. 'That would be my suggestion.'

21

A thought occurred to me. 'Inspector, were there powder burns on the man's face, perhaps in his mouth?'

Holmes shot me a look of pure delight.

The inspector didn't need to check his notebook to answer that. He shook his head. 'No, Doctor. There was no evidence of burn marks on the victim's face or hands. That is strange, and a point I tried to express to the chief inspector, but as blood from the wound might wash powder away, it isn't considered conclusive. Sir Henry did this, I know it. I just need to prove it.'

Holmes sighed. 'Let me give you some advice. If you are correct about Sir Henry, then you must work with the evidence you have. Your burden of proof is incomplete. You could never get a conviction, and Sir Henry would squash you and your career if you tried. Now, you're a bright young fellow. You know you don't have the evidence to come to these conclusions. So, focus on what you know to be true and not what you wish to be. You must give it up, you really must.'

Hargreaves thought carefully then nodded. 'You're right. I came to you to get advice, not to turn you to my way of thinking. I apologise.'

'No apologies are needed. Hargreaves, your evidence strengthens Sir Henry's innocence. With only a set of footprints, and some uncorroborated facts, a decent lawyer would tear you to shreds. And someone with Sir Henry's background and means would have the best defence lawyer money could buy,' Holmes concluded.

Hargreaves sighed. 'It is as you say.'

I had a thought. 'It is feasible Wilson shot himself and someone wiped the gunpowder off, is it not?' I could tell from experience Holmes was about to dismiss my question.

'I think it rather unlikely. It would be better to work with the hypothesis the shot came from a distance. Blood may wash off *some* traces of gunpowder but not all. Now, if the body had fallen forwards, I would agree. But it fell backwards. The larger of the two wounds, at the rear of the head. You see? The more significant blood loss to occur from there. You really must study my monograph on *flow mechanics*, Watson.'

'But surely, Holmes,' I tried.

Holmes, however, grunted and shook his head. 'No, no.'

I was not sure whether he was about to disagree with his own statement, unlikely but not impossible, or if he wished to rebuke me for mine. The answer was not long in coming.

'And why would anyone remove these qualifying marks? To do so would be to incriminate them. If one wanted the police to believe it was suicide then surely it would have been more practical to leave them? Let us move on from gunpowder residue. Notable, yes, but not significant.' Holmes raised an eyebrow, and I understood from the gesture he wished the subject closed.

Holmes thrust his left hand into his dressing gown pocket.

'Inspector, could you describe the entry and exit point of the wound exactly and precisely, please? Watson, make some notes, there's a good chap.'

The inspector found his page and began reading. As I was already taking notes, I ignored his unsubtle way of asking me to be quiet.

'The shot entered the upper jawbone on the right-hand side of his face. The ring had an abrasion, and the diameter was a little smaller than the calibre of the bullet. We have this if you need to examine it. The exit was much larger than I expected. It had an irregular shape and no abrasion rings.'

'That is as I thought. And it settles the matter. The shot was fired from a distance. Now, based on this evidence, are you still decided upon Sir Henry as the murderer, Inspector?'

The inspector rubbed his eyes.

'Now we have talked it out, no. But he had a hand in it. I'm sure of that. Still, I see the difficulties that lay ahead.'

'The danger, you mean?'

'That too. Wilson was murdered. He made an enemy of someone who then ended his life. What did he know? What did he see? Why did Wilson have to die?'

'And knowing those answers, will solve the case.'

Hargreaves nodded his agreement. But I had known my friend a long time, and it is in my opinion the sentence was not meant as a statement but a question. I frowned. Holmes read me, like he always did, and gave me an almost imperceptible shake of his head. I remained quiet.

Hargreaves said, 'There's another difficulty. Wilson was engaged to Sir Henry's daughter.'

'Ah.' Holmes leant forward. 'I take it Sir Henry did not approve the match?'

'From what I could discover, he put them together. Apparently, Sir Henry and Wilson's relationship went from being civil to hateful in short order. When I interviewed him, he said, and I'll use his words, "That young upstart shot himself, and I couldn't be happier."'

I whistled. Holmes raised an eyebrow.

'Cold, indeed.'

'I said he was a nasty sort. According to the domestics who would speak, and a number of people I interviewed around town, Lieutenant Wilson had to defend himself from frequent brutal attacks made by his prospective father-in-law. It was easy to find a few ex-employees more willing to talk. Sir Henry, they said, had publicly humiliated Wilson more than once. And here's something else. Wilson apparently never spoke up or attempted to defend his position or himself.'

Whilst the inspector was explaining, I updated my notes.

Holmes also made notes on his cuff, then went back to his pipe as he took in the inspector's evidence.

'Wilson was by all accounts besotted with his bride-to-be. It wasn't difficult to find out from the townsfolk he'd bought a lot of expensive gifts for her. According to the local jeweller, this included a rare expensive pearl set.'

'He had money then?'

'And lots of it, from what I have discovered.'

'The recipient of it, being?'

'We haven't determined that yet.'

'How was Wilson regarded in town? Was he liked?'

'Universally so, yes.'

Hargreaves sat down on the couch and waited.

Holmes sat with his fingertips together.

'So now you know why I've come,' Hargreaves said. 'Sir Henry is a close friend of the chief inspector. They play bridge with the chief constable every Tuesday night at some club here in London. Sir Henry has a government position too. I'm in a tough spot. I am convinced he had something to do with all this, but as you point out, I lack evidence to prove it. Despite being a little hot headed, I'm not so stubborn that I don't see there *could* be other answers. I'm not ashamed to admit I'm out of my depth. Will you help me?'

The last appeal would almost certainly guarantee Holmes' involvement because Hargreaves had shown he could be open-minded. My friend absorbed the information from the comfort of his seat. Knowing his methods, I imagined him walking through the events in his mind, pacing through each individual step. After a few minutes of pondering, a smile spread across his face.

'Thank you, Inspector. Your story has been most enlightening. We will of course offer our assistance in clearing up this matter for you. In the absence of more data, I beg you, waste no more time on Sir Henry. Concentrate on the household. Agreed?'

He nodded. 'You've seen something in what I've said that I missed.'

Holmes shrugged. 'You would hardly leave here satisfied had I not.' He held up a hand. 'I cannot give specifics. There are certain indications. This case may be bolder than you recognise. I will work towards helping you find a solution. I do apologise I cannot do much at this very instant. It is late, after all.'

Hargreaves chuckled. 'Of course.'

Holmes extended his hand. 'I should be delighted to make it down tomorrow. That would be convenient?'

Inspector Hargreaves nodded.

They shook hands.

'Excellent. Until tomorrow. Watson, kindly show the inspector out.'

Holmes made his way across the sitting room and stopped at the entrance to his bedroom. The inspector's face showed his pleasure and perhaps relief as he collected his belongings.

'Send me a wire with your train times. I'll have a cab pick you up at the station.' Hargreaves and I shook hands.

'Good day, Doctor Watson. I look forward to seeing you tomorrow as well.'

I looked over at Holmes, who had not moved from the doorway to his bedroom since the inspector had spoken. Holmes turned, a finger stuck to his lip.

'Answer me one question, Inspector. How has Sir Henry's daughter taken the news?'

The inspector paused, gathering his thoughts.

'Very well, I'm led to believe. She is a strong young lady by all accounts.'

'That suggests you haven't interviewed her. Curious.'

Hargreaves nodded. 'You're right, I haven't. She wasn't at the house when I got there. I later found out she left to visit her mother in Germany. I suggested to the chief inspector we get her back, but he didn't agree. "She's gone to get over the distress," he said. "Man shot himself, Hargreaves." "You're jumping at shadows." It's hard to imagine how he made it to "chief" inspector.'

Holmes grunted.

Hargreaves shrugged. 'Well, goodnight, sir.'

When I returned from showing the inspector out, I found Holmes nose deep in his index books. He muttered as he flicked through pages.

I was startled out of my musing by Holmes' vocal exclamation. I watched as he closed the book hard. When he turned, he wore a characteristic smile. Holmes spent the next few minutes studying. Anytime he seemed to find some useful information, he made a scribble on his pad. I sat watching for a time and he made another vocal exclamation and closed the book.

I half expected him to say, "The case is solved."

Mrs Hudson arrived shortly with two bowls of hot broth.

'You know, Watson,' he said between sips, 'there is something to be said for a hot broth on a wet summer's evening.'

Holmes wished me a good night, and with a twinkle in his eye and a spring in his step he disappeared towards his bedroom. A thought occurred to him and he stopped.

'This Reverend Trelean, he interests me greatly. A strange name, Trelean. Not one I've come across before. I'm sure of it. Did you know Trelean is an anagram of eternal? Why this is of any relevance I don't quite know.'

It was the final conversation of the night. Holmes turned and entered his room, closing the door behind him. I finished my cigar, drank my brandy, and ascended to my room. It was the last good night's sleep I would have for some time.

Chapter Three

It was at about four thirty the following morning when Holmes awoke me. He shook me once, smiled, and gestured for me to get up. I sat up in bed and groaned. His enthusiasm was not infectious in the morning.

'Come, Watson. We leave in thirty minutes,' he said, closing the door to my bedroom.

I washed and dressed then descended to our rooms. Holmes had a quiet primness of dress. He was clothed in a tweed suit with a black fedora hat and a silver-headed cane. He stood smoking his before-breakfast pipe, reading the Daily Telegraph. Because it was so early, Holmes had laid out breakfast. It was a disappointing selection, but I was hungry, so approached it with eagerness.

'Have you been up all night, Holmes?' I enquired between mouthfuls of toast and coffee.

Holmes flashed me an enigmatic smile. 'I have been out this morning. Where do you think I managed to get the papers from? Besides,' he said, 'sleep is a luxury I allow myself when not engaged upon a case.'

He flipped the page on the paper and something caught his eye, as he gave a loud exclaim.

'See here, Watson. If the constabulary bothered to read the agony columns, they would discover the secret to half of what is unsolved in this great city. What do you make of this?'

Holmes drew near and read aloud. 'Sir, I assume that Henry has been through the routine? I need work. Wait until all is out. Will be done and ready for payment, which should be in by the first full day to be by the clock on Saturday. It is signed *Gov.*'

Holmes looked up at me and smiled. 'I think we may have discovered a little more than our inspector, eh Watson?'

I shook my head, trying to comprehend what he was alluding to. He handed me the paper.

'What do you make of it?'

'Well, I confess upon reflection, Holmes, it means nothing to me. I mean, really, what can be meant by "first full day to be by the clock on Saturday?"'

Holmes took the paper back then cut out the section. I finished my coffee and collected my belongings, packing them into my bag for the trip to Dartford.

Holmes re-lit his pipe.

'As you are aware, I am fairly familiar with all forms of secret writing.'

Yes, I was aware. He being the author of a monograph upon the subject in which he analysed around 160 separate ciphers.

'This is not a particularly clever code,' he continued, 'and it might not have been detected had I not been looking for it. It's straightforward enough. The text contains the words "Sir" and "Henry", the solution therefore became obvious.' Holmes handed me the cutting. 'I've given you a hint. You know my methods. Let's get that brain of yours firing.'

Suppressing the urge to roll my eyes, I looked at the cutting as he requested. I tried to see past the substance of the text and look for the hidden message. Now, I do not consider myself stupid, but I confess the pattern eluded me. It appeared to be just badly worded. I was about to suggest the editor had printed it incorrectly, when realisation dawned on me. The clue he'd given me made the job simple. I saw the hidden message. My friend smiled and nodded as my face betrayed my conclusion.

'Bravo, Watson, bravo.'

The code was simple. Every third word was part of the message and it read:

'Sir Henry the work is done payment in full by Saturday.'

Holmes was quiet for a while.

'It looks like you've discovered the first link in the chain of evidence against Sir Henry. Inspector Hargreaves will be pleased.'

My friend turned and looked off into the distance.

'It does appear so, does it not? Today is Thursday. That gives us two full days to gather additional data. I have some theories that fit the facts, at least as far as I know them, but not enough to give a conclusion so early.'

'You say that as though you already have a solution in mind.'

He shrugged. 'A partial one, perhaps. Now, if you're ready?'

I nodded.

'Excellent. Then let us be off and I'll explain what I know along the way.'

We stepped outside our rooms into the welcomed fresh air. Holmes and I were used to extremes of changeable weather – England had always been that way. The morning dew settled on the road and bushes alongside our home as we walked together. It wasn't long, however, before we spotted a cab. Holmes threw his silk scarf around his neck and waved. A bright, cheerful fellow returned it and stopped beside the curb. Holmes opened the door, and we disappeared inside, our journey to Charring Cross underway.

The ride through London was uneventful. We made the six-fifteen train to Dartford at Charing Cross Station. Once the ticket inspector checked our tickets, we closed the door on our first-class compartment, opened the window, and settled ourselves in.

Holmes sat smoking his pipe with a vacant expression upon his face.

'On the face of it, the case seems simple, Watson,' he said through puffs of pipe smoke. 'I should be much obliged if you would keep a record of our findings as we proceed.'

I took out my notebook and Holmes relaxed into his seat. I was intrigued by what he had concluded from the very little evidence we had heard. So, I asked him to elaborate on his thoughts. Holmes smiled and tapped his pipe on his teeth.

'Well, as you know, it is a capital mistake to theorise with absence of the facts, but in this case, I think I can theorise a little.' He refilled his pipe. 'Lieutenant Wilson and Sir Henry were not close friends. That is clear from the house sources and from the narrative Hargreaves presented of his conversation with Sir Henry. Second, it appears Sir Henry has a good reason to distance himself from the entire affair. That fact itself is most suggestive.'

'Because he denied having found the body, even though the evidence suggested he did?'

'Precisely that.'

'We aren't simply investigating a murder, are we? Do you have reason to suspect there are more sinister motives?'

Holmes continued to fill his pipe. 'I looked up Sir Henry Wilburton before we left Baker Street. Sir Henry is a very influential and powerful man, Watson. Although he has not come under my scrutiny before, I have found several instances in my notes linking him to previous cases. Since I made those connections, I have discovered his involvement in no less than eight unresolved cases in my file. And here is the most important find. He had associations with the late Professor Moriarty and Charles Augustus Milverton; the latter may be coincidental, but it seemed less likely as I tied these facts together.'

It appeared he had done a lot more reading after I had gone to sleep.

Holmes was in a talkative mood, which meant he would impart with a lot of information. He was not always so forthcoming, but perhaps because he had not been on a case for a while, he was using me as a sounding board to ensure he had things in order. He would often say throwing ideas across to me sometimes helped see flaws in his logic. Apparently, this was one of those times.

'As I dug further, I found I had other affairs to connect him to. Including unresolved military cases and a few serious government scandals. Despite my public persona, I have not always seen a successful conclusion in every case.'

'I don't publish your failures, Holmes.'

Holmes chuckled. 'And I am grateful. The military cases were before your time. I investigated a few government cases, with Mycroft's help. Before any conclusions could be reached, they were all hushed up. The name of the official was never published, nor given to me, but I understand he was left rather burnt by those affairs. As I had records of those involved, the reoccurring factor in all of them was Sir Henry Wilburton.

'Since I was now leaning this way, I pulled out that serious fraud case we looked into last year, you remember that?'

I nodded. 'Wasn't it an internal theft or something? I remember you clearing it up.'

'Or so I thought. We caught a small fish in that instance. Again, I discovered new links. If my theories are correct, I may be able to clear up some of those cases when we resolve this one. I went down the list. It is long. His position as the under-secretary to Sir George Stiller put him in direct control of military matters. So, in answer to your earlier question, yes I do believe this case runs deeper than a simple murder.'

'Considering his past escapes, he's been rather unfortunate in this case then.'

Holmes agreed. 'It doesn't matter how careful they are, Watson. They always make mistakes. His arrogance might lead him to believe no one can link him to anything but Wilson's death. And he certainly has no reason to fear Inspector Hargreaves might.'

'And yet, he called you in to help. Perhaps you are not giving him due credit?'

Holmes inclined his head. 'Perhaps.'

'Well, your knowledge might throw Inspector Hargreaves' case into disarray.'

'It cannot. Hargreaves is a good man, but not ready for a case on this level. And I think it would hurt him too. No. We assist where we can with his murder investigation and then go our own way with Sir Henry.'

'And if he is the perpetrator?'

'I think it unlikely. He's survived through many scandals killing no one before now.'

'That we know of?'

Holmes shrugged. 'It doesn't fit his modus operandi.'

After filling his pipe and hunting for a match, Holmes stopped to smoke for a while. I watched as he stared out the window. I observed his eyes grow vacant and his expression change. When locked away in his mind he reflected no visible emotion. All it took was a case to transform him from the previous night's despairing Holmes, to the detective we all knew. Holmes remained quiet as I made rough notes on all he had explained thus far.

The light from morning was lifting the darkness, punctuated randomly by light from the small towns and houses we passed. I saw the station of Bexley and knew our journey would soon be at an end. Holmes spent several minutes reflecting, smoking less frequently and using the quietness to order his thoughts, as he often did when discarding unnecessary information. I was just beginning to think he would say no more when he spoke again.

'Now I have reflected upon various threads, the implication to a deeper hierarchy of events seems certain. I must build a profile of the young lieutenant. I am sure brother My can arrange that.'

'What will you do first?'

'As I always do. Observe and file.'

Holmes leant forward and punctuated each word by tapping on his knee. 'Consider this,' he remarked. 'The inspector has a telegram with the name Mr J Wilson written on it, not I might add, Lieutenant Wilson. Make a more pronounced note of that fact, Watson. I see from your expression you fail to understand the direct implications this mistake has offered us.'

'Is it not a trifle, compared to the entire case?'

Holmes shook his head.

'Mistakes tell me more. But I do not blame you for thinking it so. I myself in earlier days would not have considered it any more than that, but I have the benefit of experience. The inspector may show me he has a skill for observation, but I do not think he has developed to where he can isolate these trifles, as you put it, and analyse them separately. It is a common mistake displayed by nearly all official policemen. I feel sure it must be part of their initial training.'

It was a time for listening rather than asking questions, so I nodded to Holmes to continue.

'In isolation, this error is perhaps not significant. It is possible mistakes happen when one is emotionally unbalanced, yet my instincts tell me otherwise. We know something of his character. He was universally liked, enjoyed particular habits and had a great love for his bride. He was a patient, loyal man. He would not have endured abusive physical attacks from Sir Henry, were he anything else. He resisted the understandable urge to fight back. It shows remarkable restraint. All of this proves conclusively Wilson was a very balanced young man. So then, I ask you, does this sound like a man who would forget years of military service and ceremony, and overlook putting his title on a telegram?'

'The way you put it, no.'

'Thank you.'

'But I hold the retired rank of major, and I never use it.'

'Because you were a doctor first and last. And incidentally, you would never write "Mr" Watson, would you?'

'No, I don't suppose I would.'

Holmes continued his hypothesis.

'Military men do not make mistakes on matters of rank, and they don't put Mr if they have a rank. They are very keen to display their position.'

To get his point across, Holmes pulled out a collection of cards from previous clients. These cards were all on military men he had dealt with and solved cases for, or hunted previously.

'You see here these cards bear the rank first.' Holmes flipped through and found another example. 'Here, the rank precedes the name. This example shows a retired officer retaining his rank. And so on.'

Holmes put the cards back into his jacket, checking his pocket watch at the same time. He sat with the air of a master lecturer, his enthusiasm heartening to watch. He rubbed his long hands together, another one of his habits when warming to a subject. I thought the entire rank issue overstated, but apparently, he hadn't fully made his point.

'The inspector has ignored this small telegram. I shall base my case on it. If Lieutenant Wilson intended to commit suicide, why was there not a note? There is nothing in the telegram signifying his intention to do so. And, if a servant in the household were engaged to write and deliver the telegram, the mistake made on the rank would not have occurred.'

'Well, that seems conclusive,' I said, hoping it was true.

'The art is to see through the obvious and conclude from whatever remains. Trifling mistakes on notes paint larger pictures to me than footprints or bodies. Based on my conclusion, as you succinctly say, I have ruled out the entire household as the writers of the telegram. There must have been an outsider involved, who did not know the deceased was a military man. Yes, I am decided upon that fact. He wrote the telegram. He must have.'

Holmes puffed on his pipe.

'The third person?'

'Indeed, Watson. Who was this mystery person and what was the relationship?'

'You'll get to the bottom of it.'

The first rays of morning light filtered across the horizon as we talked. Holmes pulled down the window of our toxic compartment. The chilly air was refreshing.

'I will need more information before we can determine the sequence of events leading up to the murder.' He looked at his pocket watch. 'We have thirty minutes until we reach Dartford. Let us reflect in silence.'

He leaned back into his seat, closed his eyes, and smoked. I was grateful. As much as I like Holmes' explanations, I needed my own time to organise the data. I continued making notes and spent the rest of our journey reflecting upon the conclusions he had reached.

Chapter Four

Our train slowed down, and soon after we pulled into Dartford Station. Holmes, staring at his pocket watch, complained we were five minutes late. The carriage inspector gave Holmes a polite smile as we disembarked. A police cab was waiting at the entrance of the station, and after a brief exchange, we were on our way.

The station was on a hill, and from here I saw the pharmaceutical company run by an associate of mine, Henry Wellcome. He and Silas Burroughs–who five years hence sadly passed–started the firm and together they began selling medicine in tablet form, which until that point had only been available in powder or liquid. It had a profound effect on my profession, especially when they established a system of marketing directly to doctors. Holmes knew my interest and his prediction the company would do well pleased me.

Journeying past the houses of the town was a delight. Holmes pointed out Dartford had over 250,000 years of history. This was news to me. And why he knew it was also a mystery, since that level of history was not normally something he retained. As he continued, I had to assume he had done this research last night.

'There has always been a settlement of one kind or another here. There are artefacts dating back to the Stone Age. It was the Romans who established the first permanent community alongside the River Darent,' he said as we crossed to the west side of the civic populace. 'Roman Dartford, probably no larger than a hamlet, originally lay on the main road connecting London or *Londinium* with the channel ports. You look surprised.'

'I am. You rarely have any interest in matters of history, unless it is the history of crime.'

He smiled. 'But here there are people, there will always be crime. And you were not wrong. I make it a habit not to clutter my brain with useless data.'

'History is hardly useless,' I countered.

'Some, I'll grant. But come, did I not tell you some ancestors of mine once lived in the municipality?'

'No, you did not.'

Holmes continued to lecture me on the history of the proud post-industrial town.

'By 1086, when the Normans complied the *Domesday Book*, the Royal Manor of Tarentfort; the original name meaning the crossing place over the Darent, was a thriving agricultural community with a church, three chapels, a mill, and a wharf on the river. I believe in medieval times, Dartford grew into a recognisable market town with shops, inns, a priory, and accommodation for the thousands of pilgrims who passed through.'

We drew nearer our destination and Holmes pointed out various cases with connections to the town.

'The railway inauguration of 1849 brought significant changes to smaller towns all the way to the coast,' I remarked.

Holmes nodded. 'Dartford, like most towns from the coast to London, benefited from the railway. It created thousands of jobs. Local industries and new companies relocated to towns like this in the last thirty years. And along with this industrial and economic growth came more complex crimes.'

He smiled as he uttered his last sentence. I always found his macabre fascination with the worst of our society and the inappropriate glee with which he rubbed his hands when discussing it, unsettling. Our cab turned down a long straight driveway. I could see our journey's end poking up above the treetops.

Reardon House was a well-kept modernised late eighteenth century building. Under different circumstances, a visit would feel welcoming and warm. Today, with the number of police constables scouring the grounds, it seemed chilling. The cab slowed, and Inspector Hargreaves walked toward us, directing the driver to pull in near the front steps. When we stopped, Holmes flung himself out of the carriage, dropping his hat and cane in the process. I followed. Sherlock Holmes fell to the gravel and made a slow crawl examination. He looked comical, crouched the way he was. It drew queer looks from the constables, and the inspector, but I was used to it. His method of investigation must have looked odd—for odd would be a good adjective to describe some of his more unconventional behaviour—but I knew from experience it was best not to disturb him as he worked.

I had collected his hat and cane, waiting to pass them to him once he concluded his crawling around the floor. Holmes picked through small items he found, discarding some, retaining others in an envelope he'd pulled from his coat, all the time grunting to himself. Satisfied, he moved on. He continued until he reached the point at which the inspector stood and with a broad smile, he looked up.

'Good morning, Hargreaves,' he said with his usual flare for the dramatic.

The inspector returned Holmes' smile, extended a hand, helping him up.

'I hope your trip was easy, Mr Holmes?'

'Easy enough. Have you anything new to add since last night?'

He shook his head. 'Hit a brick wall, sadly. I've let the household know you were coming, but I should warn you, Sir Henry was not happy about it.'

'I imagine he had choice words on the subject?'

Hargreaves chuckled. 'That's putting it mildly.'

Holmes patted him on the arm with an uncharacteristic display of emotion.

'Omne ignotum pro magnifico, Inspector,' he said as he took his hat and cane from me.

The inspector showed no understanding, so I translated.

'What is unknown can sometimes be magnificent.'

Holmes huffed and stared off towards the house.

'That is a loose translation, Watson. Distance, Inspector, can sometimes lend an enchantment to the view. Still, in this case, I hope to have some answers for you soon enough.'

'Where would you like to start? In the house?'

Holmes shook his head. 'I have my methods. Would it be good with you if I carried my investigation without explanation until I have something to explain?'

Hargreaves nodded. 'Lead the way. I'll follow.'

'Excellent.' Holmes then marched forward, head down, and cane over his right shoulder. He moved towards a cleared path running along the driveway and stopped. I could tell he was unhappy.

'How is this?' he cried. 'The lawn and bench are on the other side of the fence and yet you have allowed a carriage to drive across the courtyard, and people to stampede over the ground like a herd of buffalo.'

'What then?' replied the inspector.

Holmes flung his arms, appealing to the sun. 'The ground, man, the ground! You have allowed others to destroy your best helpmate.'

Hargreaves did not hide his confusion. 'But I tell you the murder was committed on the lawn. The other side of the garden. What has the ground here to do with it?'

Holmes gave vent to a most dismal groan then dropped and studied the ground further. It seemed to me as though he was walking in the footsteps of some large beast, or he was measuring out the distance between the inspector's position and the line of conifers along the west side of the drive. We followed him, stopping when he did. Holmes turned pointing his cane, the sights of which were set on the bench visible through a privet fence in the adjoining garden. Holmes then relaxed his posture and made his way back to us.

'When was the body removed?'

'At nine o'clock yesterday morning.'

'Inspector,' I said, as a thought occurred, 'was an autopsy performed?'

He shook his head. 'No, Doctor, the shot was the cause of death. I didn't deem an autopsy necessary.'

'I see. Forgive me, but in my experience, it's better to be cautious. I read only yesterday a local doctor gave the verdict of heart failure, only altering it when a constable pointed out there was a bullet wound through the head!'

The inspector chuckled. 'I think we can rule out heart failure, Doctor. The cause of death was clear. I saw no need to distress the relatives further. You think this was a mistake, Mr Holmes?'

Holmes was thoughtful, then shook his head.

'No, I don't think it was a mistake. Watson is correct, an autopsy would give us a definitive cause of death, but as you say, in this instance the cause seems clear. Unless our evidence changes, I think we can move forward without one. There is still time.'

Holmes crouched again. 'You mentioned yesterday the prints going to and from the bench were Wilson's and Sir Henry's, correct?'

'That's right. If you examine it now, you'll find a few extras. The constable who accompanied me, and mine, of course. But we've kept the same shoes on.'

'Very good. And you did not notice any other prints save for yours and the constables?'

The inspector shook his head again. 'No. I was very thorough.'

'I see. Well then tell me, who in the household is five feet seven inches tall, limps with the right leg, wears steel-tipped boots with an odd squared heal, has a heavy black cane with a metal point, smokes German cigars, and has a somewhat nervous disposition?'

Holmes leant on his cane whilst he waited for the inspector to answer. Hargreaves looked at the ground and frowned.

'I have interviewed no one as you describe.'

Holmes stood and took his arm. 'Find me the man I describe and you have your killer.'

Inspector Hargreaves narrowed his eyes. 'Our third person?'

Holmes nodded then beckoned us to follow. He stopped by the fence, pointing at the ground.

'We can talk here unobserved and unheard,' he said, lowering his voice. 'Do you see it?'

We must have had blank expressions on our faces, for Holmes gestured again towards the ground. The inspector and I both dropped to our knees and looked. I noticed at once where the earth had been disturbed by a pointy-tipped shoe, and it was obvious somebody had stood there.

Hargreaves looked embarrassed. 'I can't imagine why I never thought to look here of all places. How do you conclude so much from this one print?'

'Do not feel bad, Inspector. I have been doing this a lot longer than you. Now, to answer your question, it is simplicity itself. I expected to find it.'

'I see.' Hargreaves nodded. 'We theorised the possibility of a third person, and you came to prove it conclusively. That's how you expected it. Am I correct?'

Holmes beamed. 'Very good. All I needed was the evidence to support the theory. Now perhaps you will understand why I was so vexed when I arrived. The front of this house should have been treated as though it were also a scene of crime.'

'What a fool I was. Well, I shan't make that mistake again.'

'Learn from these mistakes. They will aid you later. Now, you will remember I examined the ground from the point at which the carriage had stopped. As I opened the door, I discovered a set of tracks leading away towards the fence.'

'But how could you know a set of prints would be there?' I asked.

'Simplicity itself, Watson. The ground where our cab rests told me. You didn't notice the grooves? Forgive me, I thought it obvious. Many cabs have halted there. Over time, it has become the place they automatically drive to. The ground is worn in that location, and it had rained the night before. The impressions leading away from the harder ground became further visible in the softer. And here, they are more so.

'I observed on three separate occasions where our man rested and seemed to change his mind. The first I put down to limited light; the second perhaps a lack of knowledge of the grounds, but the third? I decided upon nervousness as the cause. Where the impressions are deepest, suggested he stopped. Perhaps to strengthen his resolve? If you look at the various toing and froing in all three spots, it alludes to a certain nervousness.' Holmes made a waving motion an inch above and across the footmarks below us.

'The impressions of his right foot were always less distinct than his left. He put weight upon it. Why? Because he limped or was lame, this lameness was supported by a cane, which had a thick pointed metal tip.'

The inspector was attentive. I had seen this demonstration of his gift of observation and deduction many times, yet somehow it still amazed me.

'You can see here ... and here where the point has left a deep impression in the ground. There are other places, but here is the best example. The shoe print, you will agree, is unusual with its distinctive squared-off shape.'

The inspector found a small pile of ash and rubbed it between his forefinger and thumb. 'The cigar?' he remarked, looking at me.

Holmes nodded.

'How is it this ash is still here? Surely the natural elements would have taken it?' I asked.

Holmes shook his head. 'We had no rainfall yesterday, and there has been no wind either. This small alcove is protected on all sides from the wind, and above by vines. We have been fortunate. And the ash itself is from a much heavier cigar. You can see here where another small pile lay undisturbed.

'The good Doctor here will tell you, I pride myself on being able to distinguish between types of cigarette and cigar ash. A German brand wrapped in straw and citrus peel. A distinctive cigar. With a unique blend of leaves, hand rolled and banded. Uncommon, expensive, and almost certainly unavailable in this country.' Holmes straightened himself.

The inspector sniffed the ash, then said, 'I refuse to believe you can tell all that from a visual inspection of ash.'

I coughed. Holmes remained stern. I expected him to go into a detailed explanation, but instead he smiled and held out his hand. 'You are correct. You can't. But if you find the cigar-end, well, that helps tremendously.'

The inspector chuckled.

'Is there any other point I have not fully explained?'

Inspector Hargreaves was thoughtful, and I could tell from the look on my friend's face he was enjoying the moment.

'The cane, how have you deduced those details? The tip I understand, presumably through the impression on the ground. But the weight and colour?'

Holmes pointed to an iron railing just visible through the fence.

'From the original railings this house once enjoyed as a separator to its courtyard, rather than this privet-hedge. If you look at the ground,' he said, pointing, 'you will see where the cane was placed and presumably fell at some point, hitting the railing.' Holmes removed his glass and handed it to the inspector. 'If you look closely, you will discover flecks of black paint which are fresh. The railing has been scored by its weight.

The marks made upon the railing have not rusted, which suggests…'

'They were made recently,' finished the inspector.

'Exactly. These facts point to the certainty this is a supporting cane, as opposed to a standard walking cane. Voilà tout.'

The inspector and I stood. Holmes had a tendency to be imperious with his deductions. The most obvious points of interest weren't always recognizable to anyone but him at any rate. Still, in this case he was instructing, and not dictating. It was a nice change. The inspector handed him back his glass and Holmes slipped it into his coat pocket.

'A very thorough demonstration, sir. Thank you.'

Holmes was not used to being praised by policemen. He was momentarily lost for words.

'So, this limping German. How do we find him?' I asked, as we followed Holmes to the steps. 'Should we put out a description of him in the local press?'

The inspector said, 'Do we want to do that? Would it not drive him to ground?'

'But if he's here, someone might see him. He has to use a cab or a train at some point.'

'No, Watson. The inspector is correct,' Holmes said from his position at the door. 'He will return. When he does, we shall have him.'

'Yes, that's right, Saturday.'

Holmes flashed me a dangerous look, and I cursed my foolish mistake.

The inspector frowned. 'What do you mean by Saturday?'

'Watson meant we have to conclude our work by Saturday, a previously arranged event we cannot avoid, I'm afraid. Although,' he said looking at me, 'perhaps upon reflection, it may be prudent to leave Watson here.'

I said no more.

My friend and I headed back towards the house. I watched with amusement as the inspector began walking in a similar fashion to Holmes, when he'd first crossed the drive. Perhaps he was trying to understand how he'd come to his conclusions. He was following footsteps we had previously failed to see, but were now obvious. Hargreaves shook his head as if to clear the thoughts and made his way over to where Holmes and I stood.

The inspector said, 'I'll have some enquiries made around the area. Local bars, cab drivers, that sort of thing.'

Holmes nodded. 'Very good. But *be* discreet.'

'And what will you do while I'm gone?'

'You work your methods, I'll work mine. We can compare notes later.'

The inspector seemed satisfied with that.

The house gave a sense of magnificence in its every detail. As old as it was, on closer inspection, it was clear recent work had been performed. There were many modern household devices, made to match the décor. The lead-lined windows with their vertical overlaid strips looked new. The front door was its nicest feature. It had the same style as that of our own in Baker Street, except it was unpainted and had a brass bell-pull and fitted with external black iron gas lamps. Holmes was on his hands and knees again. We watched as he fussed over the step.

'I want you to be careful of Sir Henry,' Hargreaves said. 'I have to tell you something. He's been onto the chief inspector. I couldn't lose your input, so I may have misled him as to your involvement.'

Holmes nodded. 'What is my pretext, then?'

'Something official, or governmental. I remember reading you have a brother who's way up there. When my chief inspector asked me how you got involved, I suggested you'd come to me. I hope I haven't offended you.' He looked embarrassed.

On the contrary, it seemed to amuse him. 'Certainly not. We shall say we were asked to look into matters as you describe. I am therefore free to use my own judgement.'

Hargreaves gave a sigh of relief.

Holmes continued his investigation. After a minute he nodded. A sign it satisfied him. Inspector Hargreaves stood with his hands on his lapels. 'Is there any further point to which I can be of service to you?'

Holmes pulled the bell and turned to the inspector. 'No. Your help has been most valuable. You will be at the police station should I need to get hold of you?' he asked with a raised eyebrow.

'Yes, I'll probably be engaged with the chief inspector for most of this morning.'

I patted the inspector on the shoulder. 'We understand. Mr Holmes and I will make every effort; you must trust Mr Holmes and his methods.'

'Oh, of that you can be sure. If Sir Henry and my chief inspector are both nervous, that's a good reason for me to be satisfied I made the right call.'

He nodded to both of us and headed to the cab.

Holmes made notes on his cuff as I watched Hargreaves' cab pull away.

'What a bright fellow,' Holmes remarked. 'You said earlier I had not given him enough credit, and you were right. I will watch his career with great interest.'

'Is there nothing of interest here, Holmes?' I asked, pointing to the doorframe. He shook his head as he pulled out a notebook and wrote something, then tore out and handed me the sheet.

'Watson, I need to get a message to my brother in the city. Since we are now playing the part the inspector has written for us, it would be prudent to have it officially sanctioned, should a question be raised regarding our motives. Could you take this to the local telegraph office and wire him for me? Wait for a reply. Do not come back until you have it.' At that moment, the door opened.

I remarked it might be prudent to interview the household staff first, but he assured me the interviews could wait. As he had disappeared inside, there was little point objecting any further. After a brief conversation, a constable gave me the directions I needed. The house was within walking distance of the town and so I set off.

Chapter Five

By the time I had left the great house behind, it was nearing nine o'clock in the morning. My mind was rife with thoughts of the singular limping man and his habits, which my friend had been able to *see* so clearly in the grounds. I picked up a brisk pace and whistled to myself as I ventured towards the historical mishmash of buildings that made up the town centre.

I had been walking for twenty minutes when I turned onto Miskin Road. The houses were large, occupied by the more affluent of the town's folk. Indeed, I understand the Miskin family were influential, playing a prominent part in the life of the town.

Later research afforded me more information about William Miskin. A respected local businessman and philanthropist. Miskin was also a member of the local board of health, not an uncommon practise for wealthy businessmen. I passed by the large fetching houses, making my way through a small connecting street, which led to the bottom end of the hill I was on. From my position, I could see I was not that far from the centre of town. The quiet suburbs were slowly replaced by industry.

I started to cross a section of road when I heard a voice call after me. I turned. A young man was waving, running down the hill to meet me. He wore light trousers and a white shirt and held a cap in his hand. I waited. Despite stopping, he continued to shout my name, as though he thought he had failed to attract my attention. At my pausing, he slowed. And it was clear by his heavy breathing he had been sprinting for some time. I noticed his youthful countenance and smooth complexion. A boy really, not much older than sixteen. He pulled at the collar of his shirt, which came away, and his face flushed red with exertion. When he reached me, he put his hands on his knees and bent over, drawing in long breaths. I detected a faint wheeze, my experience told me he was probably an asthma sufferer.

'Doctor... Watson, I...' He was still straining to breathe.

'Don't talk. Sit, catch your breath.' I tried calming him so that conversation would be possible. Initially he waved off my ministrations, but when I sternly reminded him I was a doctor, he acquiesced. That tell-tale look of panic in the eyes, as one tries desperately to stabilise one's breathing, was proof positive of his condition.

'Take slow deep breaths,' I ordered. He complied. At length he stood and smiled.

'Thank you.'

'What can I do for you, Master...?'

'Stepson, sir, Eric Stepson.' His breathing was less laboured.

'You're the butler's son?'

He nodded. 'I do odd jobs around the house.'

'What can I do for you?'

'Mr Holmes sent me. You have to return. He is in such a mood. "Do not return without him," he shouted. I ran all the way to find you.'

'Did he say why?'

The boy shook his head. 'Mr Holmes said I am to send the message he wrote you and wait for the reply. I am to bring it back as soon as I have it.'

I understood.

'You are sure you are feeling better?'

He had regained his boyish nervousness. 'Don't worry. I'll just sit here for a minute to catch my breath.'

I handed him the telegram Holmes had written.

'Remember,' I reiterated, 'wait for a reply and come straight back. No dillydallying.'

He gave me an adorable grin, and with that, I hurried back up the hill.

When I reached the house, I was exhausted. I made my way to the front and as I approached the door, Stepson – the butler whom I hadn't yet met – opened it and I was shown in. Without much conversation, he directed me to a room, and left. I entered its sombre quietness and took a welcomed seat. I had begun to calm my breathing when the sound of my friend's voice cutting through the silence made me jump.

I had not heard the adjacent door open.

'I see your old war wound is playing up again, Doctor.'

I waved my hat at him to show I was in no mood for his sarcasm.

'The walk did you some good, you seem energised.' I admit there were times when I would dearly love to wipe that irritating smirk from his imperious face.

'That was a very long detour,' I remarked. 'You sent me off as though I was a schoolboy, then sent a schoolboy to turn me around.'

Holmes nodded. 'You are irritated by your walk. I understand.'

'No. I am irritated by you.'

He was filling his pipe. 'Are you? Or is there something else?'

I sighed. 'I am hungry, Holmes.'

'Ah!' He chuckled. 'It all becomes clear.'

'Lack of food makes me hungry!'

'Lack of food makes you obstreperous, Watson.' He picked up a bell from the sitting table and rang it. He gestured we sit in the chairs. I regretted my outburst and was about to apologise when a soft knock at the door distracted me. Holmes smiled as a housemaid entered, carrying a large silver tray.

'Do you imagine I would have failed to think about your stomach? I took the liberty of ordering you a breakfast. Will that satisfy you?'

The quiet housemaid placed a pot of coffee and a plate of scrambled eggs and cold meats before me. It was the most welcome thing I had seen all morning. Not long after, she left us.

'Thank you, Holmes,' I replied, digging in.

We were quiet while I ate, and he smoked. When I was finished, I poured two cups of coffee, and we both drank as he said, 'Now you have eaten, let me detail the events of your absence.'

'First off, I have discovered a little more about Wilson and his relationship with Sir Henry,' he said, gesticulating his pipe. 'It's bad, Watson. Very bad.'

'Hargreaves wasn't exaggerating then?'

'If anything, he underplayed it.' He smoked a while longer. Then he stood and moved to the window. When he turned, he had a dark expression on his face, his voice quiet.

'I was right about Sir Henry. That snake is known to me. He locked those black piercing eyes on me the moment I entered. I am not a fanciful man, Watson, but I read the hatred in them. A man may fear for his own life at such a look, but not I, Watson. He is beyond contempt itself. Grotesque in his delight over Wilson's death. He has worked things in such a fashion I fear he will be untouchable for this crime. He also has an alibi.'

'But, Holmes. Why would he need one?'

My friend gave a tight smile.

'Forgive my ignorance, but have you not already proven this mysterious limping German shot Wilson? It seems to me Sir Henry might dance naked in the garden, and still that wouldn't change this fact. Or am I wrong?' I moved over to the window to join him.

'You are not wrong,' he said. He was distracted. Holmes then shook his head, which seemed to clear his mind.

'My, my,' he said, 'I shall get your reputation for telling a story flip-side up. Let me detail the facts. When you left, I was summoned by Sir Henry and shown into his study by the butler, Stepson. Sir Henry was seated behind his desk. He'd been there for approximately two hours given the number of fresh indentations of his feet on the study carpet, along with the number of cigars he'd smoked.

'Sir Henry had two empty coffee cups and half a bottle of brandy on his desk. I deduced at once he had worked through the night. He did not look up as he spoke.'

'"I can spare you five minutes."'

'The nerve of the fellow. He was reading a collection of papers. As I approached, I observed the customary red "top secret" stamp and the seal of the Home Office on the file. There was a business card poking out of the corner of the blotter. I suspect it had been put there that morning. Before I could get a better sense of what these contained, he folded them downward. I read something of them, and he saw that. The look he gave was a venomous one. Then with what seemed like an exertion of will, just like that, he smiled and stood.'

'"Come in, sir, and have the kindness to be quick."'

'I returned the smile but remained standing. I ran my eye of the room, and I deduced at once Sir Henry had taken precautions against any violence that might befall him. I can read the signs of a man scared for his own skin. He had no less than six weapons at his disposal. On the pretext of my introduction, I moved around the chairs positioned six feet away from his desk, taking in all that I could.

'"I know who you are." There was no mistaking his apathetic manner. "Pray tell me what the nature of your business is here at Reardon House?"'

'I explained. Concisely. He wasn't convinced about my reasons, or my credentials. "I don't mind saying this all seems a little over the top. You might find it was unwise taking on such a nonsense case."'

'There was threat in his tone. I observed him. He'd recently been in a sick bed. His pale face, a scarf around his neck, the double vest just visible beneath his shirt were tell-tale enough. He is a freemason, for rather against the strict rules of his order, he wore an arc and compass breastpin. I should say more correctly, Watson, it was a *square and compass* breastpin. The compass reminds the wearer "to keep in due bounds with mankind, particularly our brethren in freemasonry". The square or setsquare the implement with which the mason gauges right angles. He has a large signet ring, with traces of wax just visible upon it. Used, no doubt, to seal his correspondences. It bore the letters "A.V.T." It was simple enough to conclude those letters were *Audi Vide Tace*, meaning hear, see, keep silent. The motto of the freemason order.

'Freemasons, as you may know, meet in private to conduct semi-religious rituals based on the tools and practises of the stonemason's trade. It is a peculiar system of morality, veiled in allegory and illustrated by symbols intended to improve the man and offer him support in times of hardship. It is also a boy's club, Watson. A place where position in society means little. Where men like Sir Henry might find themselves junior to those with lower social standing.

'He'd been engaged in writing. For what else can be indicated by the right cuff so very shiny for five inches, and the left elbow smooth where it rested upon the blotter? These indentations were deep and fresh. The ink upon it, in places, still wet. The older sheet replaced that morning, still sat in his wastepaper basket. No household servant would be so idling in their cleaning duties as to leave such waste from the previous day.'

'"Sir Henry," I enquired, "'do you have any answer why Lieutenant Wilson telegrammed the police shortly before his death, knowing you had the advantage of a modern telephone?"'

'He creased his brow, Watson.'

"'I am not in the habit of letting people use my telephone, sir. And what young Wilson did with his time is hardly a concern for me. Frankly, I find your question an intolerable impertinence and would recommend, sir, you take heed with your tone. This is my house and you should remember whom it is you are addressing."

'He was easy to anger, Watson. "I did not mean to offend you, Sir Henry," I was quick to say, since it was not necessary to antagonise him at such an early stage. He grunted.'

"'Can you think of any reason why Lieutenant Wilson's death might be welcomed?" He wasn't prepared for that question. I could see his closely set eyes darting as he thought about it.'

'At length he said, "I cannot explain why he killed himself." He gave a pause then narrowed his eyes. "Let us not play games, Mr Holmes. If you think I am implicated in this matter, I challenge you to lay before me your evidence."'

'I came beside him and glanced at the stack of papers. Interestingly I was unable at first glance to read them. They were technical documents, very detailed. I gathered data from the more important documents and have some earlier theories validated. Underneath I noticed some private correspondences, which may have been stamped with a royal seal. He slammed the file shut, locking it away in the drawer of his desk.

'He is by no means a clever man, Watson. His late master, Moriarty, would never have been so easy to read. What had I learnt from him in that short space of time? Nothing I had not already decided upon. He's an ordinary criminal, no more or less than any other I have put away. He is no Moriarty. The rope will be too good for this one.'

'You seem almost disappointed, Holmes,' I remarked.

Holmes shrugged. 'Perhaps I have not given him due credit. He may not possess the professor's intelligence, but he did learn a thing or two in the time he spent with him. After all, I have him linked to several crimes I am, as yet, unable to solve.

'I made a decision and turned towards the window. I had a hand to play and wanted to observe his reaction while he thought my back was turned.'

'"I don't believe Lieutenant Wilson killed himself, Sir Henry," I said. "In fact, I can conclusively prove he was murdered." I watched his reflection. The result was gratifying. I turned and went for the punch. "That makes the situation different, would you not agree? After all, one does not like to hear a gentleman has had a houseguest murdered, does one?"

'Let me tell you, Watson. Sir Henry turned almost purple. He stood and took the bottle of brandy in his right hand, then poured himself a generous glass and drank the lot in one great gulp.'

'"I warned you before about your tone!"'

'I turned towards him. He shook with anger.'

'"Forgive my bluntness, Sir Henry, but why are you so agitated?" I asked.'

'He coughed and spluttered. "Why? Because you dare come into my house and accuse me of murder."'

'"I have accused you of nothing, yet."'

'"Implied then. I should have you flogged."'

'I chuckled. "I would not advise it, Sir Henry. You may think your position grants you protection from acts such as those, and perhaps a lessor man who did not understand the law, might believe you could get away with it, but I assure you," I stepped closer to look down upon his ruddy quivering face, "I am not a man you can intimidate nor coerce."'

'He backed away from me. "You are not above the law, *Mr* Holmes." His emphasis on my title was a slight, or at least he may have thought so. As you know, Watson, titles are meaningless to me. I've been offered many.'

'"Neither, sir, are you."'

'Stalemate.'

'I continued. "Did you suspect foul play?"'

'"Only you and that wretched Hargreaves think this affair has some ulterior motive behind it. It's suicide, whatever you think you can prove." He then sniffed and said, "One fact doesn't change. He is dead. And good riddance I say. Murder, suicide; it's all the same to me."'

'His misdirection was telling. I suspected him and he knew it.'

'"You surprise me, sir. If the evidence suggests murder, would you not want to discover who did this terrible deed?"'

'"No, not particularly. Why should I?"'

'"Why should you not?"'

'"I know of you. Mr Holmes the meddler. Mr Holmes, Scotland Yard's whipping boy. I have no time for amateurs, however clever they might think they are. You have no official standing. The only reason I have granted you any time today, is out of respect for your far more intelligent brother. Consulting detective indeed, bah."'

'He drank down yet another brandy, his face reddening further. He flashed me an evil glance. "If I were you, I'd stop prying into other people's businesses, consider your own affairs."'

'He was like a cornered dog, barking to scare off an attacker. His threats meant nothing. I had hit upon the truth. "Then let me say it is a great public service, Sir Henry, that you are not me." He was pacing the room, clutching the bottle. "Do you know the name Gottsreich Glacher? No? Perhaps Wilhelm von Gornstién?"'

'When I spoke that last name, Watson, he stopped dead. His face turned a nasty shade of white. Sweat began building on his forehead. I thought he might collapse. He gave himself away with his horrified expression. I had scared the bluster right out of him. He poured another generous brandy and drank down the lot. It began to concern me, should he continue drinking at every observation; he'd be unconscious before I could finish.'

'At any rate, he recovered. "I'm not clear what you're implying by dropping these names into conversation? In my professional capacity I have had dealing with several Germans. Perhaps these two names are familiar, but I cannot recall them. Who are they?"'

"'Spies, assassins," I said.'

"'Well then. It is possible I have dealt with them. As much as it pains me to say, we often trade information with spies. It's common for both sides. Doesn't your brother keep you up on policies for this sort of thing?"'

"'There can be no policy for a thing that is not officially sanctioned," I replied. He didn't like that answer. "Would you be so kind as to tell me your movements of the evening prior to Lieutenant Wilson's death?"'

'At this he relaxed. The reason for that became obvious. "Yes. I was at my club that night. I arrived at four o'clock in the afternoon, took brandy and spent the evening locked in the most riveting game of bridge. I didn't get back into the house until morning. You can check with your brother. It was he and some others I spent the night with."'

"'You are a member of the Diogenes Club?"'

"'I am. I left London on the first train out and arrived at Dartford Station around five. Stepson collected me in my carriage. I'm sure your brother can corroborate what I've told you. Now, do you have any other questions, Mr Holmes? Or may I go about my business?"'

"'I have nothing further, Sir Henry. Thank you for your time."'

'He returned the bottle to his desk. I could tell he was rattled. "Well then. Now this interview is over, I would appreciate it if you would wrap up your business as quickly as possible, then be so kind as to get the hell out of my house."'

'With that, Watson, he left the room. Such an ostentatious and conceited man, I don't mind admitting. He stormed out as a child would, having been chastised by an unhappy parent. I made cursory studies of the blotter before I left. There were things of interest. And yet...' A frowned creased his brow.

'You suspect something?'

'Yes.'

'What?'

Holmes sighed. 'Myself, chiefly. For coming to conclusions too quickly.'

I asked no more questions, for I knew anything further he had to tell, would be on his terms. I jotted down notes, articulating what I was thinking as I did.

'Suicide to murder. Complications of international concerns. European collusion? German spies, links to British government? Is Wilhelm von Gornstién the man behind the murder or is he a pawn? Was it a paid assignment?'

'Sir Henry will have had another way to coerce our German friend. You have a fertile imagination, but our thoughts are heading along similar lines. I'll need more data to make a positive decision on that. Assassination isn't Gornstién's *modus operandi,* although we shouldn't rule out anything, at least until we can rule it out.'

Holmes was facing the window. I paused my note. Something occurred to me. 'Do you think Wilhelm wrote that note in the agony column?'

Holmes smiled. 'Yes, I'm sure of it.'

'So that suggests he was paid to kill him?'

Holmes laughed. 'However did you jump to that conclusion?'

I frowned. 'Well, was it not something like, the deed is done? Full payment by some clock on Saturday? Seems clear to me. It confirms he killed Wilson then claimed his payment.'

'It does nothing of the kind. Why did Sir Henry not just pay him afterwards? They were both here?'

That stumped me. 'I have no answer for that.'

'I do. The deed was something else entirely.'

'What direction do we take now?'

He turned, pipe jutting out of his mouth, hands thrust deep into pockets. 'The least dangerous, I should say.'

Holmes drew three or four pulls from his pipe. As I finished my breakfast, satiated by the food and energised by the coffee,

I looked up to catch a twinkle in his eye. He pulled his pipe away, dreamily rubbing its worn tip across his lips.

'Was there more to your encounter than you've let on?'

Holmes collected his thoughts. 'I left the room with more knowledge than I had before entering it.' Holmes checked his pocket watch and returned it to his waistcoat.

'That's the best answer you have?' I asked.

He shrugged. 'For the moment.'

'Have you examined Wilson's bedroom yet?'

Holmes nodded. 'I left the study and Stepson showed me to the room. He is a guarded and well-practised man to be sure, a credit to his station. I made comments on the relationship between his master and Wilson, but Stepson shrugged them off with a blithe look. I probed him and he admitted to some arguments between them, although he was not prepared to offer any details. But without telling me anything of importance, he did by his actions convince me of his guilt regarding the treatment of Wilson. Stepson has something to fear in his master. That much is obvious. Is it possible he knows the circumstances that led to Wilson's tragic end? Possibly. Like so many trusted servants, he would have the better understanding of all that happens in this house. Still, without facts, or evidence, I can prove nothing. No jury will convict a man based on my ability to read his body language. No matter how good I am at doing so.'

I felt Holmes underrated his abilities, but he seemed comfortable with what he had said.

'I examined the room, but there was nothing of real value there. It seems to have been picked clean by the police. I did discover Wilson had written a letter that morning, addressed to the officer in charge of his regiment. But the details on the blotter were masked.'

I looked up. 'By Stepson?'

Holmes shook his head. 'No, by Wilson, who was reasonably clever although not enough to foresee his own demise.' Holmes pulled a section of blotter from his inside jacket pocket. 'You can see the indentations here.' He ringed them with his finger. 'They are distinctive. A careful examination with the glass reveals the paper was pushed into the blotter on each stroke of the pen until the main body of the letter was written. A torn corner of the blotter tells me he used it to cushion between his letter and the blotter which explains the missing body of the text.'

Holmes finished his pipe and emptied the contents into an ashtray on the small mahogany table adjacent to my seat.

'That's suspicious in itself, isn't it?'

Holmes was cleaning the stem of his pipe. 'No, not entirely. When people like Milverton will turn even the most trustworthy servants with a cheque-book, this suspicious behaviour, as you put it, becomes ordinary through necessity.'

He was of course referring to *Charles Augustus Milverton*, the notorious blackmailer who had the blood of many fine young men and women on his hands. Thankfully no longer. Still, there will always be secrets and scandals. And that meant there would always be another Milverton around the corner.

'How did you discern who the recipient was?'

'He made a mistake on the first envelope and threw it in the trash.'

'Do you know if the letter was posted?'

Holmes shrugged. 'I asked Stepson if he handled the post that morning. He said he had. Did he notice a letter from Wilson? No. But as Wilson went for a walk, he could easily have posted it himself. Given his concern that the details should not be read, it seems logical that he would not trust a servant to post it. I will check with his regiment when we get back to London.'

'Should we examine the site of the murder, now the police have left it?'

'It would be instructive to run our eyes over it. If only to dot the Is and cross the Ts. Once we have our data, I suggest we make our way back to London for afternoon tea.'

'Sounds good to me.'

Holmes filled and relit his pipe and smoked for at least ten minutes in complete silence, while I continued to write as much as I could, enjoying the coffee.

I was reflecting on the conversation and underlined points I was unsure of. Who was Wilhelm von Gornstién? German obviously. Nevertheless, what did it suggest? We'd had dealings with blackmailers and spies in the past, and from what I had gathered from Holmes' details—albeit limited—the case had taken on a 'European' nature. The indications signified a more harrowing and reprehensible affair.

'There's something familiar about all of this,' I said to Holmes as I put my book away.

'Indeed. Put aside the murder for an instant, and given the government ties, I think it's a path we've walked more than once.'

'You mean like the Naval Treaty Affair?'

Holmes nodded. 'Since Sir Henry works for the Secretary of Defence, Watson, it can't be a coincidence.'

'No, it can't.'

'Well, I promised the inspector an answer before the day was out. I have the foundation of a case and most of the players mapped out. A few threads remain and those I can only investigate in London. I think it would be useful to telephone him and let him know where he can contact us.'

After I had gained permission to use the telephone, I made the call.

I followed Holmes through the house's west wing. Holmes' eyes flicked from pictures to doorways. He occasionally stopped and looked out through a window. When we reached a newly constructed sunroom lacking furniture and other adornments, he stopped again. Once he had taken in all he could, we exited onto a charming secluded patio.

It was a bright, warm, cloudless day. The picturesque garden expanded before us. There were several well-tended flowerbeds. The pride of some meticulous agricultural genius no doubt. I was never blessed with a green thumb, so was envious of those who could keep such beauty tamed and contained. Being early summer, it was a great joy to see the flowers in bloom, adding colour and excitement to the otherwise dull green of the lawn. The trees were full of leaves. The grounds gave a feeling of tranquillity. In other circumstances, the house would have been a wonderful haven or retreat.

'Aha!' said Holmes, dropping down and examining the collection of walking boots arranged alongside the large, ornate metal boot cleaner.

As Holmes studied the boots outside by the door, a man in clergy regalia approached us. This had to be the Reverend Jeremy Trelean. I recalled the inspector telling us of his frequent visits.

He was a small man around five foot five. Soft of skin and clean-shaven, with silver swept back hair. He had a nervous look in his eye and he made no eye contact with either of us.

'Good morning, Reverend,' I remarked with a lift of my hat.

'If you say so,' he replied with a dark look.

His response surprised me. 'I did not mean to offend you.'

Realising his impudence, possibly, he took my hand. 'Forgive me, I have a lot on my mind. The death of Mr Wilson has caused all of us a lot of pain.'

Holmes looked up, his eyes narrowing. 'Mr Wilson? Surely you mean *Lieutenant* Wilson? You are in positive danger of dishonouring his memory by your poor choice of words. Reverend Trelean, isn't it?'

Trelean looked puzzled. He held a questioning gaze upon his face. The trifling *faux pas* of rank usages emerged its head again. Holmes suggested the individual who wrote the telegram may have been the same person who committed the crime. But could this clergyman be involved? It seemed unlikely. But I could not dismiss that Holmes had remarked that an omission of this nature would not have been made by anybody who knew the murdered man. Perhaps there *was* something more to this stone-faced old reverend? In any event, Trelean now came under Holmes' scrutiny.

'You have me at a disadvantage, sir?'

'I am,' said Holmes, 'Sherlock Holmes, which may clear up that point.'

'Not for me it doesn't. Never heard of you.'

'Obviously no great reader,' Holmes muttered aside to me.

'What was that?'

'Nothing, my good Reverend, nothing at all.'

Holmes had a curious expression. The reverend narrowed his eyes for a moment, then softened his features.

'I do not need to be reminded of poor *Lieutenant* Wilson's actions. May God forgive him for his terrible sin.'

He made an effort to break from Holmes' gaze and it struck me as though he was irritated at being held up by our conversation.

'Well, I'd better be getting on. May God bless you, sir.'

Holmes stopped him and his manner became more curious. It's sometimes difficult to describe to you the way he can change personas, and one can never fully appreciate my friend's uniqueness for facial expression, at least not in print. It could best be described as somewhere between quizzical and sceptical.

As was Holmes' usual way when he needed to gain more information on his subjects, he started asking questions to provoke reaction, with less concern for the response.

'One moment, Reverend. Perhaps you can assist me with something before you go?'

'What is it?'

'A simple enough task. Can you tell me which set of these boots belongs to Sir Henry?'

Trelean frowned then shrugged. He made a study of the boots, then picked up a set.

'This pair has "HW" on the rim inside, seems like they'd probably belong to Sir Henry.'

Holmes, I knew from experience had looked the man up and down twice. I observed those quick glances of his.

'You impress me, thank you. Now before you go, how long have you been in the service of Sir Henry?'

With this, Trelean smiled. 'I never have been in the service of Sir Henry. I am a man of the church, Mr Holmes.'

'Ah, my mistake.'

'Should I go now?' he asked.

Holmes looked quizzical, then smiled. 'One last question. Have you ever been to the United States of America?'

The reverend laughed. 'No, I don't travel.' With a curt nod of his head he left us.

Holmes returned the nod and said, in almost a whisper, 'Interesting.'

Holmes put a finger to his lips and smiled. His eyes followed the old clergyman until he was out of sight. He realised I had questions and pointed to a large hanging willow tree in the centre of the lawn, gesturing for us to proceed to it. I followed but not before I caught the glaring face of Sir Henry Wilburton watching from one of the bedroom windows.

Chapter Six

Holmes and I crossed the lawn in silence. As I followed, he made studies of footmarks and dropped to examine impressions and collected bits and pieces I honestly couldn't guess what level of importance he placed on them. I took a deep breath filling my lungs with sweet air in abundance all around me. Holmes remarked he would be happier once we had left the fresh, healthy country air. It hid, he said, a sinister undertone. At least in London, the smog and industry matched the criminal elements of our capital city. He wasn't wrong.

It seemed our destination was a large clump of trees near a dilapidated summer pavilion. Holmes' route must have taken us twenty minutes. I could have walked the entire grounds at least twice in that time. I was glad when we were in seclusion under the long hanging branches of a willow tree.

The birds sang songs above us. The shade was a welcome respite from the hot mid-morning and I made a quick sketch of the grounds from my position. The bench where the horrible affair took place was visible. Holmes scrutinised it from the distance, waving his stick towards the house and back on more than one occasion. I could see the fence from which the man Holmes described had probably shot Wilson. I could make out the small path running alongside the house up to where it met the fence.

I stood in silence admiring the view. Holmes continued his work and when he had finished, pulled out a pair of cigarettes and lit them both. Handing me one, he leaned with his back on the tree and whistled.

'This case, Watson, this case.' He had a slight frown. It suggested he had not found what he had been looking for. Holmes had a wonderful appreciation for minuscule details. I remember a case where he determined the time of death of a murdered dignitary by the length of time butter had been left on the table from breakfast. He had bought the same butter, made conditions the same as they were at the scene and timed how long it would take the butter knife to sink through, as it had done when the victim in that case had died. He performed four tests with the same results each time. The defence argued the entire experiment was nothing more than theory. A jury disagreed.

'I think it best if we went back to London. I don't imagine I can learn anymore from here.' He finished his smoke and flicked it away. Then with a look at the house, he tapped his hat with his cane and indicated for us to go.

'Shouldn't we at least wait until your telegraph is answered?'

'If we've had no reply by the time we leave, we can relieve young Stepson of that task.'

'Holmes,' I remarked as we walked away, 'what was it you were looking for in the lawn? You picked up odd items as we crossed.'

'All in good time, Watson. You shall hear and see enough by the end of today. Now come. One last examination of the bench and we can leave. That will give us plenty of time to catch the thirteen forty train back to London.'

With that, we came to the bench. As we approached, he stopped me and handed me his cane. I watched him perform his usual scrutiny of the ground. He left nothing unturned, on some occasions took out his glass. Twice he made comments about police officers being herds of elephants and the greatest bunglers of all, but he did not stay too long at any one spot. It was as if he knew there was little to be gained from being there.

'Well, one thing is confirmed. Sir Henry never approached the bench.'

'I thought the inspector said Sir Henry's prints were positively matched?'

'They were.'

'And you've proven otherwise?'

'Not in the least.'

'Then I do not follow. Those boots walked this lawn, correct?'

'In the manner you're suggesting, no.'

'Boots can't just walk a lawn without someone in them, Holmes.'

'Exactly. But who says they have to be worn by their owner?'

'Someone other than Sir Henry wore his boots?'

'Stepson did.'

My mind clouded over. It seemed as though we were getting further from the truth.

'The butler, are you sure?'

'Utterly. Stepson has six-inches on Sir Henry.'

'Which means what, exactly?'

'Small men do not leave stride marks indicating them to be six-foot in height.'

'Unless they are attempting to fool you?'

Holmes gave me a look. 'You mean to say, Sir Henry, conscious the police might call to investigate, made it appear as though someone else was wearing his boots?'

I shrugged. 'It is possible.'

Holmes considered me. 'Did he disguise his dominant side to throw me off as well?'

I had no answer.

'I do not mean to offend.' Holmes beckoned me to a crouch. 'See, the indentations made by the left foot are more developed than those of the right. It suggests left-handedness. Sir Henry is right-handed. Did I not tell you he picked up the bottle of brandy with his right hand? Take that and his height, Stepson is the logical choice.'

'But why would he attempt to implicate Sir Henry walked this lawn?'

'That is a very good question. Was he instructed? Or did he have his own motives?'

'Shall we not ask him?'

'There would be little point.'

I looked at the ground. 'Holmes, you really are amazing.'

He waved his hand. 'It was nothing.' But I saw the smile of appreciation on his face.

Holmes took his cane from me. We moved off in the direction of the path and from there made our way around the side of the house towards the front driveway. As we rounded the corner, young Stepson came to us. He held the reply to the telegram Holmes had dispatched me to send earlier.

'Well done, Stepson. Here's a sovereign for your trouble.'

Young Stepson's eyes widened. 'A sovereign! Thank you, sir. Mr Wilson only gave me a shilling.'

Holmes gave him a sharp look. 'Mr?'

The boy, lost in his reward, failed to recognise the implications of what he had just said. I however beamed, turning to Holmes. Before I could say anything, he put a finger to his lips and scowled.

'Not a word, Watson. Not a word.'

We did not have to wait long before a cab arrived and took us directly to Dartford Station. I wondered if that young man understood he had unwittingly thrown Sherlock Holmes' deduction by his youthful mistake? I put it down to a change in society. I could not draw Holmes on the subject and the issue of ranks and titles did not come up again.

When it was safe, I asked Holmes what the telegram had said.

'It is from Mycroft. He writes: "Can confirm Sir Henry's movements of the evening in question. Have some thoughts on the matter. If convenient come at once, if not convenient come all the same."' He didn't say much more.

After a small wait, we boarded. The first-class compartments were full, so with two other passengers, we entered the second-class carriage. As the conductor blew his whistle, the door opened and Reverend Trelean got in and walked past us to a seat further down the carriage. Something about the man bothered me, but I could not say what it might be.

'You see, but you do not understand,' said Holmes interrupting my train of thought.

'I beg your pardon?'

Holmes indicated the reverend with a quick movement of his eyes. 'Our clerical fellow is an agent for the British government.'

'Good Lord, Holmes! How can you be so sure?'

'The British Agency have provided spies with a special railway ticket for use across Great Britain and the continent. It would be unusual were they not to take advantage of it. Now, when I see a clergyman travelling first class, my suspicions are raised; when I notice the knees of his trousers do not shine, my suspicions positively levitate.'

'Knees?' I said, not knowing whether he had made the observation in the carriage, or before when he studied him at the house.

'You do not see the connection?' Holmes asked. 'Forgive me, I thought it obvious. Reverend Trelean may pray, but not I suspect for his eternal soul, and certainly not in the conventional position. Perhaps you noticed. No, what am I saying? Of course you didn't. Trelean has a callous on the index finger of his right hand.'

'And?'

'It's indicative.'

'Of what?'

'A familiarity with firearms of which any leading member of the church would hardly approve.'

'I should say so.'

Holmes smiled and crossed his legs, sinking back into the chair of our carriage.

'There were other indications you, as a writer, should have picked up.'

I did not understand what he was suggesting.

'He lied about his having travelled. He has without doubt spent time in America.'

'I wondered why you asked him that.'

'His use of past tense and auxiliary verbs gave him away. "Should I go now." Does that not sound foreign to your ears?'

I thought about it. 'I suppose I would have said, "Shall I go."'

'Of course you would have. "I never have been." Really.'

'How you pick up on these things is beyond me. So, he followed us?'

Holmes nodded. 'Oh, he was clever about it, but he never left our side from the moment we ventured towards the station. I observed his boots when we entered the carriage; naturally, he was our cab driver. He stalked us and watched our movements around the house. Perhaps he concluded we would leave and went on ahead. I imagine he had a cab ready nearby. Once he dropped us off, he gave us time to enter the train and dispense with his disguise. His entrance precisely timed for the unobservant so it would appear he left after us.'

'Well, this whole affair is stranger and more complex with each passing minute.'

Holmes smiled at me. 'You think so?' he said, stretching out on his chair. 'I find it to be refreshingly clear. I require a few more facts and the answers to three questions and I shall have the case concluded.'

I studied the reverend trying to see if it were possible for me to ascertain his motives. Holmes fell asleep for the remainder of our journey and I pondered on what had been discovered thus far.

I note from a reader's perspective, it would be easy to lose track of all the facts discovered. Sir Henry, a known consort of Professor Moriarty, was involved somehow in the affair. Holmes concluded Sir Henry was aware of Wilhelm von Gornstién, a German who he believed shot Wilson. It tied in with the cigar discovered at the scene. The motive for murdering Lieutenant Wilson was unclear, and no prompting from me could force Holmes to elucidate. There was the unknown European element tied in with the German assassin. So, was it a case of discovering the whereabouts of the murderer? Or was it important we find out what motive led to organise Wilson's death? I thought the former, but Holmes believed the latter.

Holmes' remarks about the papers on Sir Henry's desk. He said they were technical documents that were difficult to read. Were they in code? If they had been in German, he would not have made the observation, as Holmes spoke the language fluently.

Holmes' brother Mycroft confirmed Sir Henry had been with him on the night before Wilson's death. Perhaps Lieutenant Wilson had discovered Sir Henry had been in association with the late professor? But that didn't fit either, because Moriarty's crimes were never made public; to this day his family still protest his innocence. I suppose it was plausible Wilson discovered some underhand wrongdoing by chance. But was he blackmailing Sir Henry? It did not fit with what we knew about him. But it might answer the question of his wealth, which seemed too large for a man of his station. If he was using blackmail, might that not lead Sir Henry to take drastic action? But then why a German? Why not a local ruffian? These were questions I would not have answers to for some time.

Something else sprang to mind as I watched the towns flash by on our journey back to London. Trelean. Was he a

British agent as Holmes had surmised? Or was he a villain engaged by Sir Henry?

I turned my eyes up the carriage to find him, but he was gone. One thing was very clear. I decided it might be safer if I stayed awake for our journey home.

It was at about mid-afternoon when we finally found ourselves in our old rooms in Baker Street. The day had been long, and I was famished. Mrs Hudson had seen to a light snack, before she made up our table for dinner. Holmes disappeared into his bedroom returning with his mouse-coloured dressing gown and a relaxed expression. He stood over the fresh fire and pulled some tobacco out of the old Persian slipper. I poured tea and gestured for Holmes to join me.

'Tea, yes, but I cannot allow myself the luxury of food. The digestion process requires too much of my energies. No, I shall sit here with my pipe and ponder on this pretty little problem.'

I drank my tea and ate the cakes Mrs Hudson left; it seemed a shame to waste them. I then retired to my faithful chair by the fire, lighting my afternoon pipe. It was not long before I picked up my notebook and made another pass through the events of the day.

Chapter Seven

I must have dropped off during my writing because I was awoken by Holmes' exclaiming jump.

'Watson! I am a fool, a first-rate idiot. I have bungled my way through this simple affair like so many of those poor dullard police officers I am quick to decry. What has happened to the brains God has given me!'

'Have you discovered something new?' I asked, while stifling a yawn.

'We have been looking at this all wrong, or rather, I have. I fancy Hargreaves was on the right track from the beginning. I put Wilson's death down to nothing more than a ploy. A sleight of hand, as the theatre magicians say. Designed to point us in one direction in order to direct us away from something more sinister.'

'That seems to be the direction in which we have been investigating,' I agreed.

'But what if I am wrong?'

'In what way?'

'What if Wilson's death was not deliberate as I first suspected?'

'You mean he *did* kill himself?'

Holmes shook his head. 'He was murdered. If his death wasn't meant to misdirect … perhaps it has a different significance?'

'You mean, it wasn't planned?'

Holmes smiled. 'You have it. Consider this. Sir Henry is in London the previous evening. He comes home early the next morning, and not alone. Somewhere along the line our German friend, Wilhelm, joins him. When they get home, within two hours, Wilson is dead. A singular coincidence, wouldn't you say?'

'Meaning no coincidence at all?'

'You see it? So now we ask, why was Wilson murdered?'

'Maybe it was an accident, and they were simply covering it up?'

Holmes shook his head. 'You think this German was taking pot shots at seven in the morning? In a secluded part of the privet, firing haphazardly into the garden?'

'When you put it that way, it does seem unlikely.'

'No, no. They are collected by Stepson from the station. Perhaps he informs Sir Henry that young Wilson was seen in his study. He has written a letter addressed to his commanding officer. Stepson knows this and offers to take care of posting it. Perhaps they have a discussion about it? Wilson not trusting Stepson makes a pretext for posting it himself. Needing some morning air, or some such conversation, he walks it to the post box outside the property and deposits it, secure in the knowledge that only a postal official could remove it.'

'Now what must Sir Henry think when he hears this? A man who has many secrets. He must surely become suspicious. What has Wilson seen? Why has he written a letter and posted it himself? Whatever the motivations, and no matter how innocent Wilson's letter may have been, that is the reason I think Wilhelm killed him.'

'Because of what he may have known?'

'Exactly.'

'The poor fellow. But that implies Stepson was part of this conspiracy.'

'Well, he may not have pulled the trigger, but he *is* complicit. He's been Sir Henry's butler for nearly twenty years. How can he not be? Something new was in that house, Watson, and whatever it was, Stepson knew about it. That sealed Lieutenant Wilson's fate.'

We were interrupted by a knock at the door and Mrs Hudson entered.

'A gentleman is here to see Mr Holmes.'

'No, no, Mrs Hudson. I cannot see anyone else. Tell him to come back a week on Tuesday.'

'He is most insistent, sir. A very official-looking gentleman if you ask me.' She handed Holmes a card.

He raised an eyebrow as he read it. 'Official?'

She nodded. 'Like someone who might work for the government.'

'Interesting. This card tells me nothing, which piques my interest enormously. Very well then, please send our visitor up.' Holmes crossed the sitting room and collected his clay pipe from the mantelpiece.

A moment later, he was standing in our sitting room.

Our visitor was an elderly man with regal stature. He was, as Mrs Hudson had suggested, a gentleman. He displayed a well-groomed moustache and close clipped silver-grey hair. He wore a suit of fine quality and held a large top hat with a band of blue silk. It was a made-to-measure style, the type you would see in Savile Row, where the finest hat makers in London reside. A man of means, then.

He was well built, standing over six feet tall. He was stockier next to the lean frame of my friend, and his face was kind. His intelligence was reflected through bright hazel eyes. Holmes gestured for him to enter, taking his hat and cane, and hanging up his coat on the hook outside the door; a practise he performed when he wished a closer study of his visitors.

Holmes waved his hand to the settee. 'Please be seated. This is my friend and colleague Doctor Watson whom you can trust.' He then dropped himself into his favourite chair.

'Now then,' he said as he looked over the card once more. 'How can I assist you, my Lord?' At my friend's use of a title, our visitor's eyes widened.

'How the devil...'

Holmes chuckled. 'I assure you the devil had nothing to do with it. Observation is a gift of mine, a gift that has prompted your need to visit, I assume?' Holmes filled his pipe and lit it.

Our visitor seemed uncertain.

'I can see an explanation is in order. Like all arts, the science of deduction and analysis is one, which can only be acquired by long and patient study. It is possible to learn at a single glance the history of a man and the trade or profession to which he belongs. A man's fingernails, his coat sleeve, by his boots or by his trouser knees, by all these things a man's calling is revealed.'

'You handed me your cane on entry and I observed it had the crest of the House of Lords upon it. Your sleeves were clean and free from shine, so one might assume you were not a clerk, but a man of some importance, as you have with you the strongbox of a government official. You have also neglected to remove the cleaning tag from the inside of your jacket. Wilkinson Co. a popular firm used by many Parliament officials; there is a small note attached inside marked for delivery to the House of Lords main entrance. I do not for a moment believe you are employed to deliver cleaned suits. You are a member of said organisation, rather than a servant of it.'

'You wished to remain incognito?' Holmes asked raising an eyebrow at our guest, who gave a slight inclination of his head.

'I see. That must be why you tried to mislead me with this false card?' Holmes' facial features became stern and after a brief study of the card he returned it to our guest.

Our visitor nodded once.

'It is as you say, Mr Holmes. Believe me, it was not my intention you should have been given the wrong impression at all.'

'Then it was another who suggested it?'

'Ordered it, would be a better way to explain it. You were wrong about one thing.'

'Oh?'

'I am a servant of the very organisation you deduced. As any member of the House of Lords should be.'

Holmes nodded. 'I concede.'

'I've come to you, on the advice of the Prime Minister himself. He explained you are of impeccable character. You have helped to assist him on a few occasions with, as he puts it, flawless precision and the utmost care. I desperately need your services. I cannot go to the police in this matter, for to do so would cause such a scandal the likes of which this country has never seen, nor possibly recover from.'

Holmes and I looked at each other. 'Might I have your full name?' Holmes asked, offering the cigar box.

'Lord Peters,' he replied, removing a cigar and clipping off its end. Holmes snapped the box closed. Our guest and I jumped.

'No, no. If we are to conduct this interview any further, then I will require your real name. I am used to having a mystery at one end of my cases, but at both ends is far too confusing. No, I must ask you again for your full name?'

'Very well, Mr Holmes, but understand you put me in a serious predicament. For you, sir, with all your cleverness may do harm to me just by knowing it.'

Holmes cocked an eyebrow. 'I will do no such thing. For if I can work with scandals for kings and queens then I am sure I can do the same for you. Now, your name?'

Our guest sighed to himself.

'Very well, Mr Holmes. You leave me with little choice on the subject. What I am about to tell you is and must remain in the strictest of confidence. My name is Lord Montague Henry Défarrus.'

He settled himself down and he recounted his story.

'I have been engaged for the last six months on behalf of Her Majesty Queen Victoria to liaise between the royal households of Germany and Great Britain. I was also instructed to maintain and keep safe certain documentation, which are of a critical and private nature to Her Majesty. I controlled this with the help of Sir George Stiller the Secretary for Defence. We had procured in secret a strongbox and locked certain royal documents away in the parliament vaults.'

Lord Défarrus lit his cigar, and I noticed, as did Holmes, the brief way his hand shook.

'Pray continue, my Lord,' said Holmes after offering him a glass of brandy.

'Thank you. On Monday of this week a document from certain foreign parties found its way into the royal correspondences and communiqués. I realised it was not for Her Majesty's personal eyes, and so opened the letter to determine its content.' Défarrus took a large sip of the brandy. Holmes refilled his glass, and he continued.

'Well, I don't feel it necessary to explain all the details, but let me just say it was a letter which had been addressed to the Queen of England. The writer was not named in the letter, but the general contents referred to several personal correspondences between the German government and the British aristocracy, which could indicate a sympathy for the possibility of a Great War involving all of Europe. A situation occurring with more frequency lately. With this in mind, the government has set-up a specific course of action to deal with such occurrences.'

'I take it blackmail is what we are talking about then,' I said after making a note of what His Lordship had said.

'I fear so, Doctor.' Défarrus took another sip of his brandy.

Holmes stood up and paced the room. 'Did the envelope have any sender address information? Postmark? Something that could indicate where the letter had originally been sent?'

'No, Mr Holmes, the envelope had been hand delivered. It was a one-penny sheet of ivory Foolscap paper, torn along one side and folded along its centre. The writing was in indigo ink and apart from that I can offer no further information. Frankly, Mr Holmes, this situation is grave. For if these correspondences were to become available to the public, the scandal could take us to the brink of war.'

I had seen my fair share of war in Afghanistan and was against any conduct that could help initiate the possibilities of another.

'Lord Défarrus, there are some points I need further information to. Why have you waited until Thursday afternoon to consult me and what has been done to track down the writer of this letter?'

'Excellent questions, Mr Holmes, the worst was discovered this morning. I entered the vault to collect important documents and found the box opened. I established that four papers had been removed. I questioned Sir George, but he was as perplexed as I.'

Holmes was thoughtful for a second. 'Can you describe to me the contents of these documents?'

'No. I am constrained from doing so.'

Holmes' irritation flared. 'Can you at least describe them? It might be hard for me to take on such a task without at least some details.'

'The documents were written on cream-coloured paper, watermarked by Her Majesty's own paper manufacturers. Sixteen inches in length and ten inches in width, all tied together with a single strip of purple silk, and stamped with the royal coat of arms.'

Holmes lit his pipe.

'Thank you. And now let us discuss what was contained within.'

His Lordship rose and I could tell that he wrestled with the seriousness of this problem. He looked over at me and I saw a deep regret in his wild eyes. Panic seemed to pass across his face and then almost disappeared, as he regained his composure and sat back on the settee.

'Very well, Mr Holmes. The delicate nature of these documents constrains me from explaining their full content, but I can tell you certain phrases could bolster sympathy within a small group of the Prime Minister's political adversaries. The publication might escalate such feelings to a point where those who seek to topple our government, might succeed. If that should happen, dire consequences may be unavoidable.' His face distorted to despair, and he pulled at his watch chain.

Holmes frowned. 'Surely you exaggerate? Explain to me how the scribbled indiscretions of a letter possibly topple a government?'

'The Prime Minister's position is not as secure as you might think,' he replied. 'You take me into the dirty pits of political opportunism. There are dangerous intolerant men lurking in the corners of Westminster who desire to lead Great Britain into a new age. One free of European influences. One where just being the balancing scales within an armed camp is not enough. Her Majesty is aware of the precarious position these poorly thought-out letters put us in.'

'Who would benefit from these documents?' I asked as Holmes scribbled on his notebook.

'Aside from those I have just described? Any of the great chancelleries of Europe, Doctor.' Défarrus dropped his head on his chest and sank into the settee with a heavy heart.

Holmes was thoughtful. 'How would weakening the Prime Minister achieve this?'

'A general election is imminent. If they are published before it, the scandal would energise opposition and the Prime Minister would have no recourse but to resign. That would leave the country in the hands of those bent on British dominance.'

'You were correct to come to me as soon as you did. I assume your agents have made a detailed search of the vault? I will need their findings as a matter of urgency. What is Sir George's position?'

Lord Défarrus looked at my friend and without blinking he replied, 'Sir George knows less on this matter than you now do.'

Holmes nodded. 'Apart from what you have described, what is so idiosyncratic and vitally important about these particular documents?'

Défarrus looked down towards his shaking hand then his steel nerve reasserted. Holmes made a gesture of continuation and he nodded. 'They are written in the hand of Her Majesty, when she was a much younger woman.'

Holmes puffed his pipe furiously for a short time. 'I think we can act for you on this matter. Watson and I are engaged on another vital case. We should be able to give it our full attention whilst employed on both.'

Lord Défarrus shook his head. 'The other case cannot compare to the seriousness of this. I would be far happier if you put all your energies into this one.'

Holmes smiled as he drew on his pipe. 'And yet, that is surely my decision.'

Our visitor inclined his head. Holmes and I stood as our illustrious client rose. I collected His Lordship's belongings and handed them over. He looked to Holmes.

'You know where to contact me should you have any fresh developments. The staff of my agency are also at your disposal.'

'Regarding your agency. There is a question I should like to ask, and please be frank with your answer. It could have some bearing on the case.'

'Ask away,' Lord Défarrus said.

'What do you know of the Dartford incident?'

Défarrus gave a puzzled look. 'I have no knowledge of any incident at Dartford, should I?'

'There was a murder on Sir Henry Wilburton's estate yesterday morning. You were not aware?'

At the mention of Sir Henry, I thought I noticed a slight scowl appear on his Lordship's face. It was gone in an instant. 'No, I assure you.'

Holmes nodded. 'Forgive me, but I was sure one of your agents was working the case.'

He shook his head. 'I have no agents on cases in the suburbs. Typically, we don't involve ourselves in matters the police have jurisdiction over. Perhaps you are mistaken, Mr Holmes?'

Holmes nodded. 'Yes, I must be. Well, good day, my Lord.'

With the last remnants of our conversation over, he left the room, closing the door behind him.

I was eager to consult my friend, but waited for Lord Défarrus to leave. When the door to our rooms had closed, I moved across towards the window to watch as our client entered his carriage. He paused at the door and turned back to look at me. I smiled and offered him a wave as he entered the carriage and closed the door.

Holmes had turned towards his bureau, making some notes of his own.

'Holmes!' I exclaimed, barely able to contain my excitement. 'The two cases are linked, they must be.'

'The faculty for deduction is clearly catching today,' he said, chuckling. 'Calm yourself, Doctor, and sit down, man, you're like a jumping bean.' Holmes held a humorous expression upon his lean angular face.

'Well, Sir Henry works for Sir George Stiller. It all makes sense to me now. These documents must have been what you examined on Sir Henry's table when you interviewed him. Why, we should go down there now, and horse whip this fellow for his obstinacy.'

Holmes fell to his knees in laughter and I must admit to feeling a little annoyed by it. Holmes waved me to sit and when he calmed himself, he wiped tears from his eyes and spoke.

'My dear Doctor, you have a most singular wit. I do not laugh at your suggestion, my dear friend. You are correct in your deductions. However, we cannot jump to any conclusions regarding the aforementioned documents.' Holmes took a long pull on his pipe.

'I think we can settle the matter of Wilson's death, and should answer the question of what was new in Sir Henry's house.'

'What do we do now, Holmes?' I enquired.

'We will keep this latest information to ourselves for now. I must speak with Mycroft. He will give me the answers no official agency can. Then, I fancy, a visit to the police library.'

'What about this agent?'

'Ah yes, we must not forget *Reverend* Trelean. A wildcard. I have not made up my mind about him or his involvement. It is curious.'

'Do you think Lord Défarrus was lying?'

Holmes thought for a moment. 'No, I believe him. *That* is the curious thing.'

He left around seven o'clock and I settled into writing up my notes.

Chapter Eight

It was late evening when I finished writing the last sentence of the day's adventure, that Mrs Hudson came in with a letter addressed to Holmes. As he was not in, she handed it to me. It was from Norwood, so probably not linked to our current cases. I turned it over a few times to see if there was something that I could read from it. There wasn't. So, I dropped it onto Holmes' bureau with a shrug.

Mrs Hudson had been watching me, and she smirked.

'Trying to deduce who it's from, eh, Doctor?' She winked at me. 'Another case, perhaps? The mysterious affair of the evening post!'

I offered her a tight smile, as she collected the remains of my supper.

I was about to pour another drink, when there came the most hideous commotion from downstairs. We rushed to the top of the stairs to find Wiggins shoving an elderly person out onto the street.

'I has to see Mr 'olmes. It's vital, you young ruffian!' he bellowed in a deep cockney accent, waving his stick around.

'Mr 'olmes ain't in at present. If you wants to see 'im, make an appointment.' The boy had almost extricated him when I intervened.

'It's okay, Wiggins. Send the visitor up.'

The boy shrugged and allowed the old man into the hallway. 'See? Little rascal,' he said glaring at Wiggins as he re-entered. He then hobbled up to the stairs after me. It appeared as though he was afflicted by arthritis in both legs. I could tell from his stiffness and the loss of joint range of motion, that the left was more crippling than the right, since he favoured his right side more. He was around sixty, with a ruddy complexion. He struggled halfway up our stairs and stopped for breath. He also had a rattling cough. The journey up, I mused, might be the last one he made.

'One … one moment, sir,' he wheezed to my questioning gaze. I assisted him in finishing the journey upstairs.

'Thank you, sir, thank you muchly. Mr 'olmes, I presume?'

'No, my name is Watson. Doctor John Watson. I assist Mr Holmes in his investigations. Maybe I can be of help to you?'

The old man seemed most disgruntled.

'Well, no h'offence … but I ain't got no time for assistants. It was to Mr 'olmes that I was to give information to. I knows about Dartford, right? And I 'eard a reward being offered, right? But I 'as me own important stuff going on, so I'm not about to waste time in waiting. How long is 'e gone for?'

He was obstinate and guarded. He also never left his grip on his stick or hat.

'I expect him shortly. You may tell me all, I assure you. I have his full confidence. If you wish, sir, you may well regard me as his close advisor and partner.'

He let out a laugh. 'Not bloody likely. I'm off.' He made a movement towards the door. I don't know why I decided it was best he stayed, but once I'd decided, I stopped him. He had a wild look in his eyes.

'You can't keep me 'ere, it ain't right? Stand aside, I say, or by the devil himself, I'll …'

He held his chest and bent over with that rattling cough. I helped him to a chair.

'Sir, you are not well. Please, I am a doctor. Rest. I assure you Mr Holmes will be back soon. Remember there is promise of a reward.'

'Seems fair, tho I ain't in no moods for confinement.'

I turned away towards the door and thought it best to lock it, taking the key and placing it in my waistcoat pocket. I moved across to the sideboard and poured myself a brandy. When I turned around, I almost jumped for gone was the wheezing old man, to be replaced by my old friend. I should have known better.

'Watson, you may at least offer me a drink,' he said with an expression of deep agitation.

'Holmes, you rascal. What was the meaning of the disguise?'

I poured Holmes a drink and he sat in his favourite chair. The clothes he had abandoned lay on the floor next to him. He swallowed the drink in one gulp. I replenished his glass and he seemed to relax. As he settled, he removed the last vestiges of his disguise. It was only then I noticed his left hand was wrapped in a bandage, crimson with blood.

'Well, my dear Watson, the criminal world is somewhat alerted to my presence since you published my cases. I had reasons for wanting certain other parties to think I was elsewhere when in fact I was here. I had a scuffle with some ruffians. I would be obliged if you could put your skills into effect, and attend this wound.'

I examined it. Although it looked bad through the blood-soaked bandage, it was superficial. 'You're lucky. It doesn't look infected. I must clean it, and it will hurt. How did you come by it?'

Holmes winced as I dabbed cleaning agent upon it. It was a clean cut, about five inches, and running the measurement lengthwise of his hand up to the joining section of the lower arm. From the angle of the wound, and the length of it, I gauged it had been from a fixed blade.

'It looks to me as though you were attacked with a bayonet, judging from the bruising and the angle of the cut. It's not too deep, you were lucky.'

Holmes looked at me with admiration.

'Doctor, your observations are accurate. Two men approached me just as I was leaving the Diogenes Club. One, six foot three with a steady aim, as you can see by this, but no other skills. Both German. The other, our limping murderous friend Wilhelm.'

I continued cleaning his wound as he continued his story.

'We had a small conversation and then they attacked. I dispatched Wilhelm easy enough, knocking him to the ground first. That wheezing fool had no chance. The larger of the two was the real concern. Despite his size, I was able to employ my Bartitsu skills to subdue him. I had almost got the upper hand, when he pulled out the rather curious knife that inflicted this wound. Before he could murder me, I was saved by our silver-haired agent who fired a shot at them. Both ran quickly after that. I thanked him as he helped me up, and examined and dressed my wound. He said very little. Careful!'

I ignored his outburst and he continued sourly.

'He at least was mindful of the pain of it.'

I chuckled and continued my work.

'I am not a fanciful man, Watson, as you know, but had he not intervened, I am sure you'd be reading about my death in the morning papers. Trelean, for that is the only name I have for the man, had been tailing either me or my assailants. What little he would say, suggested they were sent by Sir Henry. When I asked him if he was friend or foe, he cocked his head and said, "I haven't decided." He then assisted me to Mycroft's house, and left. At this point I have decided he is a friend, for he could have easily left me to be hacked to death.'

'Well then, thank goodness for him.'

'Indeed.'

'Were you able to discover anything about him?'

Holmes shook his head. 'Nothing, Watson, and it irks me.'

'Because you haven't been able to observe anything of value, as you can with others?'

Holmes said nothing more, but I felt I had hit upon the true reason.

I finished cleaning his wound and applied alcohol to kill off any infection. I then re-dressed it and Holmes thanked me.

'How did you know they were German?' I asked as I cleaned my hands.

'Because, they spoke in German,' he replied sardonically. Holmes found his pipe and filled it with tobacco.

'I observed our rooms being watched when I left, and when I arrived in my disguise the same watchers were still there; although, I fancy they failed to recognise me as you did.'

I poured Holmes another drink but he waved his hand. 'I need my mind sharp.'

'It appears Sir Henry has got you in his sights.'

'Possibly. But I have no data to validate that. If Sir Henry is the kingpin, I'm rather disappointed by his poorly conceived plan.'

'Not that poor, since had Trelean not been there, you'd be dead.'

Holmes gave a slight shrug. 'Maybe *that* was the plan.'

'What do you mean?'

'Well consider this agent, or whomever he is. The shot he took was unobstructed and clear. So, was it meant to warn rather than kill? Why? If he is as precise with his marksmanship as he is with his other skills, then one if not both should now be dead. Did he need them alive? Were they co-conspirators? And if so, was the entire thing stage managed and he the organiser?'

'Perhaps he simply doesn't like to kill.'

Holmes gave me a look.

'Surely we have a good reason to go to the Lestrade?'

Holmes finished filling his pipe, now settled in his favourite chair.

'You forget Lord Défarrus' small, but nonetheless important part of this puzzle. No. As with Professor Moriarty and his gang, if we act too soon, we risk losing a larger group in favour of a smaller one.'

I rose from my chair, retrieving my discarded book from the table. Holmes found a match and lit his pipe.

'Was Mycroft helpful?'

Holmes chuckled. 'That rather depends on your definition of the word helpful.'

'He had nothing of value to give?'

'Mycroft doesn't work that way. At least not with me. It's always an exercise between us. He gives me problems, I offer solutions. I've said before, when it comes to the art of deduction and observation, Mycroft is the better. But despite these exercises he and I favour, they start with a mutual sharing of knowledge first. Afterall, it is no fun attempting to problem solve when one is missing vital data.

'Sir Henry is not the idealistic imbecile I initially thought him to be. His associations with the freemasons have given him a lot of cover and the scandals that are known, are buried too deeply to hurt him. Mycroft suggested there's no sense in beating that dead horse. I tend to agree. Mycroft also relayed the official position of the government over him; one of caution and unease. They have nothing to base any real reason to dismiss him. We heard today, groups of men like Sir Henry have political association who conveniently intervene to save him. The Prime Minister and his allies bemoan their colleagues lack of guile in finding ways to deal with him. So, they move him from assignments they are hopeful will curtail his disreputable acts. Which of course it doesn't. And to make matters worse, they heap additional responsibilities on him in anticipation the workload forces him to resign. Which he won't.'

'Why there should be different rules for members of government, is beyond me.'

'Politics, that's the answer. The implementation of the law remains in the hands of the police, who are constrained by parliamentary procedures and by privileges set in the chamber. Let us also mention the police are directed by the Home Office, and with Sir Henry's influence, he could ensure any investigation fell across his desk.'

'The average person is afforded protection under the law, but not to this level. It's wrong.'

'It's historical and entwined into our system. It will take some future brave souls to tackle it and succeed. Corruption on this scale, sadly, is usually top down.'

'You can't mean the Prime Minister?'

'Why not? He's a man elected into office. Aside from his privileged upbringing, he is no better or worse than any other citizen. Just as able to commit the same crimes you or I could. The only difference being, whilst in office, it is a lot harder to prosecute him without it appearing politically motivated. Therein lies the scale of the problem.'

'I understand. I still don't like it.'

Holmes puffed on his pipe for a moment and then said, 'Do you remember the poor Agricultural Minister Sir Peter Davies-Hope found dead not two years ago? Mycroft had Sir Henry fingered for it. But again, because *no scandal* is far more preferable to a conviction, what evidence they might have had, was conveniently lost.'

He sighed.

His melancholy did not faze me. It always amazed me how deep my friend would go, to find facts in the most difficult of places. I would not want to be in Sir Henry's shoes, for all the money in the world. Professor Moriarty failed to appreciate the full and varied talents of Holmes, and for that matter so had a great many other villains. It seemed each time my friend was called upon to assist in some official case, the criminal never understood what it meant to be hunted until he was on them.

He would find a way to get Sir Henry, I had no doubt of that.

Sir Henry Wilburton was a fool to try to outsmart Sherlock Holmes. I had just discovered however, it would be a difficult task to touch him, especially with all the support he had. Sir Henry could not see past his own greed and grotesque accomplishments, yet his arrogance meant he could weather it all with impunity.

Holmes continued.

'I know now this affair was perpetrated with a single most vicious reasoning. Lieutenant Wilson discovered what Sir Henry was up to. Had he come to me it is just possible he would be alive to see the fruit of his labour. But instead he sealed his fate. You remember he wrote to his regiment? Well, the letter did get posted. Sir Henry can thank Stepson for that blunder. In it he detailed several things he had observed or been witness to. His letter said he intended to confront Sir Henry over what he wrote as, one step too far. And now we know why Lieutenant Wilson had to die. But there is some light to this dark affair. Sir Henry's actions have ensured he will face a far more serious problem. One he might have assumed he would have protection from.'

'What is it?'

'Not what, Watson, who.' His features turned hard. 'Me.'

Chapter Nine

I poured tea, and we sat in silence while we drank. Eventually Holmes put down his cup. 'The police could have investigated Sir Henry for a hundred years, and would have come up with nothing.'

'You said it yourself, Holmes. You had more data than Hargreaves. Because of that, you could link Sir Henry to things in ways the inspector never could.'

Holmes nodded. 'It is true. Sir Henry has been far bolder than we first imagined. During my interview with him, he talked about Wilson's death as though it was right and justified. Sir Henry's amateur attempts to remove me from the case has strengthened my resolve. Hargreaves was right to question the motive behind Lieutenant Wilson's wife-to-be scuttling off to Germany.'

'It is understandable to think Lady Wilburton grieves and would want to visit with her family. Naturally, if her mother lived in Germany, then it isn't unreasonable she would go there first. We know she didn't murder Lieutenant Wilson, Wilhelm did. Why this sudden postulation regarding her?'

The keenest expression played upon my friend's face. I also noticed the sparkle had returned to my old friend's eyes. 'It is the positive link in both affairs. Don't you see?'

I had to be honest and say I didn't.

'Let us leave that aside for one moment. You say she grieves, I say, if she grieves, Watson.' He smoked for several minutes, blowing great clouds of smoke into the room.

'How many times have I told you to look past the obvious? Who is the mother? Sir Henry's wife? Why is she living apart from him? These are the questions we need answers for. Why is she protecting her daughter? And why did her daughter pack up and leave when her future husband was being murdered that morning? Who is Trelean? What is his connection to this affair?'

'Holmes, I thought she went away because he died. You're suggesting she left before?'

'I am.'

'How could you know all of this?' He had piqued my curiosity.

'It was not a difficult thing to comprehend. She's Sir Henry's daughter. She knows everything about his affairs.'

'But how can you know? She may not share her father's penchant for criminality.'

'I admit, I have no evidence to back up my claim. Call it experience if you will. Like all master criminals, they need underlings to perform certain tasks that are not linked back to them. One might postulate he trusted her over an employee? She's a University graduate with linguistics degrees in German and English. Has a double first in law. Given what we already know, how can she be anything but her father's most trusted advisor?' Holmes kicked off his shoes and slid on his slippers. He then pulled out an envelope from his inside pocket.

'Here is a very interesting letter, dated two years hence. To a certain Peter Davies-Hope, remember him? Do you know our poor girl has been so unfortunate, she has been engaged to marry no less than four members of high society, only to have them all kill themselves just before the ceremony can take place? What shocking bad luck.'

I could not hide my surprise. 'That's damning evidence. How did you come by it?'

'I bought it, off a servant.'

That appalled me. 'You did what?'

Holmes smiled through the smoke. 'I'm aware of the irony, Watson. Unlike the Police, I am not constrained by procedure, nor and am retained to supply their deficiencies.'

'But you are constrained by the law.' I was angry, and he knew it.

'And what law have I broken?'

'I don't know. But it's underhand and devious.'

Holmes gave me a critical look. 'It is no such thing. We've broken the law together, on a few occasions, Doctor. Why turn squeamish over this?'

I couldn't articulate why I felt what he'd done was wrong. 'It's ... well, it's wrong.'

'Nonsense. Pull yourself together. I've offered to buy material before, to save a client from blackmail. Why is this different?'

He was right. 'I suppose it isn't.'

'Exactly. Now stop being so obtuse. What do you imagine I was going to do with it anyway? Turn into a blackmailer?' He chuckled, and his smile broke the tension between us.

'Let us move on. Consider the facts Lord Défarrus laid before us. We have a known consult of Sir Henry looking after documents of a secret and personal nature for the Queen of England. We also have a man charged with the secret plans for this country's defence, Sir George Stiller. What would happen if a war were declared tomorrow? The Defence Secretary and all his top military advisors would be around a table, discussing strategic contingency and deployment plans. Once finalised, they would be presented to the Prime Minister. Her Majesty would be consulted, and the usual practice of commons vote on the legalities that precipitate any actions which might take this country to war. Once passed, the House of Lords creates an act, we'll call it the "War Act", which makes a war legal.

'Her Majesty is consulted, who remains apolitical and signs the document as she is constitutionally obliged to do. The Prime Minister and his cabinet then make all the necessary preparations for war.'

'That I understand, but what are we saying? That war is inevitable?'

'Yes. I believe it is. Maybe not today, or tomorrow. But it is coming, Watson. Mark my words.'

'And you think Sir Henry has somehow manoeuvred the entire government and monarchy into a war, all by himself?'

'Not by himself, but yes. I believe that is what is happening here.'

I was aghast. 'But surely if we can find those papers?'

'We might stave off a war today, but if four pieces of paper can be destructive enough to provoke one, we are already there. It is really just a matter of time.'

'We must do everything we can to get them back.'

Holmes gave me a sad look. 'That might prove difficult, as I believe they are already on their way to Germany.'

'But how can you know this?'

Holmes leant forward. 'They went with Sir Henry's daughter, of course.'

He allowed me time to process what he had said.

'It's a mess of a conspiracy,' I said. 'I can't see how we can possibly act.'

'The situation isn't entirely hopeless.'

'Well, that's a relief. You suggested Sir Henry wasn't alone. Are you saying he too is just a pawn?'

'Not quite. He's not a puppet, but there are people in the background, pulling strings, Watson. One thing is clear, at least to me. Only one person could have given Sir Henry the key and the authorisation to go to the vault. From there he could take any documents he would like.'

'But how would he know which ones to take?'

'Elementary, my dear Watson. Sir George Stiller told him, of course.'

'The Secretary of Defence?'

'Oh, yes. Sir George is as much implicated as Sir Henry. Think, Watson. The Premier himself is unaware of the potentially dangerous position Sir Henry now occupies. It hardly bears thought at the damage he could do, whilst employed by Her Majesty in the Defence department, especially if war occurred. But as we know this document was shrouded in secrecy, the only way he could have known about it was from Sir George.'

'What about Lord Défarrus?'

'I considered that, but Mycroft disagreed. He paints a very dull picture of the man. As he puts it, "The man is incapable of the lack of moral fibre one must exhibit to enact high treason".'

'He struck me as a man of integrity.'

'He is. A model government employee with drive, passion, and honesty. As I said, dull.'

'Then whom do we go to? We can't just call in on the Prime Minister and say, excuse me, sir, but your Defence Secretary and members of his staff are traitors.'

Holmes pulled another drag from his pipe and smiled. 'But, my dear Watson, that is precisely what we must do if we are to stop it.'

I sat down and contemplated what Holmes was considering.

'What could be in those documents that could cause this level of scandal? War is a nasty business, Holmes. I have been through my fair share, and I don't think this country is prepared for it, not so soon.'

My friend agreed but I could tell there was more behind his unemotional façade.

Holmes lapsed into silence. The room felt a little colder for him doing so.

'Have we been so outsmarted, the chase then has gone cold?' I asked with a fearful dread in my heart.

Holmes shook his head which lifted my spirits, if only slightly. 'I wouldn't say that. We may still yet be able to recover the original documents.'

'I'm relieved and yet confused. Because you just said they were already on their way to Germany.'

'Did I?' Holmes said with an innocent expression I didn't care for.

'You know damn well you did.'

'Well, perhaps I mislead you a little. Do you not recall I told you Sir Henry was a master forger?'

I did recall it. 'Of course. So, the original document might still be here in England?'

'It is possible. If forged copies were on their way to Germany, they will become useless should the original be recovered.'

'How so? Surely the scandalous nature of them won't change?'

'But they won't be able to be authenticated. A forged document of that nature will be seen as nothing more than a hoax.'

'We hope.'

'We hope, indeed.'

I regained the optimism I had lost. 'What's our next move?'

'There is only one man in London bold enough to play this game. Hugo Oberstein.'

Those who keep up with my case notes will remember my publication of the case of the Bruce-Partington Plans. This scandalous and deeply dangerous affair put the plans of the Bruce-Partington submarine into the hands of this treacherous villain. The conclusion of the case earned Holmes the emerald pin from her Majesty. We both thought the affair finished as Oberstein was given a sentence of fifteen years. Alas, an unscrupulous barrister used a technical loophole in the law to secure his freedom. It was a sad day for the family of Arthur Cadogan West, the brave man who lost his life trying to recover them.

'I would have thought we had seen the last of him,' I said at hearing his name mentioned again.

'I fear not, Watson. This case affords him some very high stakes which I am bound to say, attracts him a rather handsome price. He could not turn down such an intriguing offer, since he was ruined financially. I realised the connection when I saw the documents on Sir Henry's desk. He had not yet finished copying them when I interrupted him. You may recall I told you a business card was in Sir Henry's blotter? What I failed to mention was the card was Oberstein's.'

'Let's go and arrest the fellow right now,' I said getting up from my chair.

'Not so fast, dependable Watson. We have a game that needs playing first. Oberstein is of no use to us, not yet. We have time. Either Lady Wilburton has the originals, or Oberstein does. The balance of probabilities suggest she has them and she'll take them to Oberstein soon enough. When she does, I'll have them all.'

The night had drawn in and the fog started its slow roll down the street. As I listened to the everyday sounds of cabs making their way through the streets of London, I contemplated the horrible possibilities that war would bring. Would marching armies storm London? Westminster? The palace? Would our proud country fall?

I turned my mind to brighter thoughts, of gentle fragrant flowers blooming in the spring meadows, honey bees going about their daily routine unhindered by man, and birds singing sweetly in the trees. These were things that made life so wondrous, not the wanton destruction of human beings by other human beings.

Holmes broke in upon my thoughts.

'Watson, a chill has come. Throw another log on the fire, would you? There's a good chap.'

I did as he instructed and sighed. It was a peaceful evening by a fire. And while joy and happiness crept from my mind, I held tight to the thought if anyone could find a solution to this terrible problem, it would be Sherlock Holmes.

'Well, what are we going to do about this mess?'

Holmes seemed to think about this for a time, and then a brief smile formed across his face.

'Chin up, man, not all is lost. We will prevail, it is natural to think of the worst cases in these situations, but positive thinking must shine through. At any event, there is no guarantee war would break out over this scandal. The government and Her Majesty would do everything within their power to resolve things, with no need for bloodshed. We must rely, therefore, on the purview of diplomats.'

I couldn't tell if he really meant that, or was saying it for my benefit. But somehow, it eased my mind.

There was a tap at our door and Mrs Hudson came in.

'Mr Holmes, Inspector Hargreaves is here from Dartford. He wishes to see you urgently.'

Holmes smiled. 'Good, I was hoping he would come. Send him in, Mrs Hudson.'

He turned to me. 'Go with me on this, I need to extricate ourselves from any further investigations of Lieutenant Wilson.'

'Of course.'

Mrs Hudson showed Inspector Hargreaves into the sitting room. He removed his long overcoat, saying, 'Gentlemen. Mr Holmes, I got your message, thank you. Now you must know my career is in the balance. If I have nothing to go back to my chief inspector with by morning, I will be out of a job.'

'Well, we can't have that!' Holmes offered the inspector a seat and poured him a brandy.

He took the drink and sipped it. 'You were very helpful before, but I hoped I could get something tangible to clear things up.'

'Then I will give you something. A German man, aged thirty-two, named Wilhelm von Gornstién, murdered Lieutenant Wilson. The facts are simple. There was an argument between Wilhelm and Wilson at some earlier point, probably over money. He may have discovered Wilhelm was up to no good. Wilson had Stepson's son send a telegram to fetch the police, so he may explain whatever impropriety he was accusing Wilhelm of. And out of revenge, or possibly fear, Wilhelm shot him whilst he sat on the bench. Sir Henry found the body as you described. It's all there.'

'Do you know where this German is now?'

'I have made inquiries, but alas, no.'

'How did you discover his name?'

'As you know I have a good recollection of historic crime. I searched the police archives and found Scotland Yard wanted a man matching his description for a similar crime. In fact, two. I discovered an international warrant for his arrest in France, Belgium, and Austria. If you take this photograph to the station master at Dartford, I am convinced he would be able to give you a positive identification. All the data is there.'

Holmes looked at me and I did not betray him. He'd left out vital information pertinent to our case, but not to the inspector's. It was necessary to be half truthful when what was at stake could blow all Holmes had worked towards. It made my previous disapproval over Holmes' purchasing of the letter seem, well, juvenile by comparison. The inspector sighed in relief. He thanked Holmes, who handed him a file of evidence. I don't know when he'd had the time to put it all together.

'You understand, Inspector, I do not wish to appear in your report or this matter at all. You have determined all this for yourself through deductive reasoning and careful planning, and I pointed out a few theories, but you worked and solved the case. Are we agreed?'

'As you say, sir. Thank you. With this fuller description and all this physical evidence, I will catch this villain and he will hang for his crimes. What about Sir Henry?'

Holmes said, 'I will handle Sir Henry. You concern yourself with Lieutenant Wilson.'

Hargreaves rubbed his chin in thought. 'There's more to this, isn't there?'

Holmes remained neutral. 'You have your information, Inspector.'

Inspector Hargreaves narrowed his eyes. After a moment he nodded, and they shook hands. Holmes wished the Inspector success in his search.

'Mr Holmes, I first approached you in this matter with an arrogant over ambitious opinion of myself. I thought I could solve this case and make you see not all police officers you've had dealings with are poor investigators with no initiative. I realise my mistake and I thank you most sincerely. Your reputation, sir, is considerable. I will do as you ask, but I feel it only just you should receive some credit. If not now, at some point in the future. Therefore, when the doctor takes up his pen to write this case up, I will stand up and be counted.'

Holmes smiled. 'You will go far in your profession, Inspector. You can see there is more to an investigation than the narrow view certain facts can lead you. But you must always look deeper. Especially at the trivial and the obscure, for these can tell you far more than bodies or footprints. Crime is common. Logic is rare. You may not always succeed, but if you use logic and imagination, you will better your peers every day of the week. Goodbye, Inspector.'

After he had departed, Holmes relaxed. 'I wish him success, but he will be looking a long time for Wilhelm. International spies don't stay long once discovered.'

'What about the spy on the train? Reverend Trelean or whatever his real name is. Why was he involved? His actions make little sense, now you've explained things.'

Holmes leant forward. The firelight gave his features a sharp edge, as the flames flickered.

'Well, there we move into the realms of conjecture. I erroneously put him down as a British agent. I am still at a loss to explain his presence, although I have suspicions.'

'Such as?'

'A discussion for another time.'

The black-hearted business was beyond anything I could imagine. Nor could I fully comprehend the scale of this deep-routed corruption existing within the government of the country I was so proud of. How far did it go? Somebody had to deliver the letters to Her Majesty by hand. This was incredible and terrifying. To think anti-European unscrupulous objectors were capable of closing in on the Sovereign. And the Prime Minister. Unthinkable.

In all the years and on all the cases my friend and I worked, this affair gave me my darkest and foreboding memory. Holmes tapped out his pipe.

'Perhaps he thought his true purpose uncovered? When he followed us, he must have known I would see through him?'

'You said he was working for us, or at least, not an enemy. Maybe he's trying to get the documents back as well?'

Holmes turned his head in my direction, a frown forming. 'You suggest he was engaged by the sender to recover these documents?'

'Why not?'

'Why not indeed? Interesting. I had not considered that. It does makes sense. Let us go with that as our official answer until we have reason to discount it.'

We sat for a while in silence and then Holmes stood.

'Well, my dear fellow. We have a long arduous day ahead of us, and so I will bid you goodnight.'

With that, he retired and I also, for I was completely exhausted.

As I undressed for bed, I thought of the possibility of failure. I pulled the covers up as I lay to sleep, but sleep did not come for some time. I could not seem to disengage my mind from all everything Holmes and I had discussed. Coupled with the echoes of the terrible thoughts I'd had earlier, if we were too late in retrieving the original documents.

Eventually, I drifted off into a disturbed sleep, my dreams full of images of war.

Chapter Ten

I awoke the following morning with a start. It was nine o'clock, and the sun shone through the gap in my curtains. My suit was laid out beside my bed and a bowl of hot water was ready for me in my bathroom. I washed and dressed then left the room, making my way down into our sitting room.

The room was tidy. Holmes was sitting at his table working on some chemical experiment and when I entered, he jumped up, smiling.

'Ah, Watson, splendid. Did you sleep well?' He seemed delighted to see me. It made me suspicious.

'Not really. I had a restless night. Most of it spent thinking about the horrors of war.'

'And for that I apologise. We should probably find other topics to discuss before bedtime. Especially for you, with such an impressionable mind.'

I ignored his sarcasm. 'This case has frightening undertones; I shall be pleased once it is concluded.'

Holmes nodded his agreement.

'However, all that can wait, since my stomach thinks my throat has been cut.'

I made my way over to the breakfast table and poured myself a coffee. The Times lay in its customary place, and I picked it up and read the morning headlines. I was contemplating it, when Holmes broke in on my thoughts.

'I agree with you. The government should be more productive in spending the taxpayers' money this winter,' he said, joining me for breakfast. I looked over at him, amazed by his observation. I could not fathom how he had concluded what I was thinking.

'It was not difficult,' he replied to my look. 'I simply observed you'd read the headlines, "Government to supply funds for newly established museum." And I agree with you, that there should be more money available to the elderly or to the supply of gas to every gentleman's house in winter. You seem disturbed by my observations,' he concluded, sitting down next to me.

'Is mind reading a new skill added to your arsenal?' I replied, turning the paper over.

Holmes laughed. 'Hardly that, Watson.'

He studied me for a little while longer. I lowered the paper and sighed. 'Are you going to let me in on the secret?'

'It is no big mystery. I did not for one moment suspect you were interested in the latest lady's fashion for summer, which is, by the way, the other headline printed on the section of the paper you are reading. Your expression of aversion was obvious and you have so often remarked at how much of the taxpayers' money is wilfully misspent.'

I laughed but caught myself in time before I made some off-the-cuff comment about how absurdly simple it all was. Better to just be amazed and move on. Still, he was wrong about one thing. I was interested in the latest lady's fashion, but then Holmes being a calculating machine, would not recognise that.

Holmes yawned and stretched himself upright, reaching up and almost touching the ceiling.

'How are you feeling this morning?' I asked as he poured a coffee.

'Very well, actually. I must admit I was reasonably tired last night. The exertions of the previous day took their toll, but I am suitably refreshed now.'

'And your arm, how is that feeling?'

'Sore, of course, but healing. I am grateful for your ministrations.'

'I will redress it when you have time.'

He thanked me again.

Holmes began to demolish the large plate of toast.

'I'm glad to see you eating, although you usually don't until a case is concluded.'

Holmes nodded. 'True. But I confess I find myself with the need to replenish energy. I am not as young as I once was.' As he made for the jam, a thought occurred to him, and he pulled an envelope from the pocket of his dressing gown.

'This is the letter that arrived yesterday.' He tossed it onto the table in front of me. 'I found it on the sideboard this morning. You must have forgotten to give it to me. I cannot blame you; it was a rather busy night. Tell me, what do you make of it?'

I picked up the note and studied it. It was a curious letter and I shall write it as it was written to us.

Dear Mr Holmes,

I understood you have bean taskd with investigation of the death of James Wilson, who resides at Reardon House, Dartford, Kent. Pleese back of, sir, or be trodden underfoot.

U ave been warned, take heed.

Very sincerely yours,
A Friend

I read and re-read the letter in disgust.

106

'This is surely a threat, no doubt from some bounder employed by Sir Henry?'

Holmes winked at me. 'Yes, it most certainly could be, but it is also a very encouraging step forward in this affair. Give me your observations.'

I examined the letter but saw nothing of importance in it.

'Well, the person who wrote it is ill-educated,' I said at once. 'You've had your share of threatening correspondences. Considering the kind of people Sir Henry surrounds himself with, it's possible he has a madman in his employ. It must have come from him; I should give it no further thought.' I put the letter down and continued to read the morning paper.

Holmes replenished his coffee and placed the pot back down on the table.

'My dear Watson, your command of the obvious is, as always, nonpareil. The world is full of mad men. What can *you* deduce from it? What does *this* letter tell us about the writer?'

'I am not sure,' I confessed, 'aside from the poor spelling, I see nothing.'

Holmes grinned. 'On the contrary. You see everything, but you fail to observe. However, all is not lost, as we are getting somewhere. You observed the peculiar spelling, splendid. Doesn't it strike you as informative and suggestive?'

I had many observations, most of which centred around my opinion of his imperiousness at breakfast. However, it was clear I wasn't going to get to enjoy my paper, so I swallowed my irritation and played along. 'You're suggesting whoever wrote this is trying to appear less educated than he is.'

'She is.'

Incredibly after all these years, Holmes still managed to startle me. I could not grasp how he'd concluded, from the limited information, that the writer was a woman. He must have seen my undisguised disbelief because he smiled and indicated to the letter again.

'I could give you a long explanation on my study of handwriting, which is most instructive as to a person's character and, I am convinced, gender. But I recognise your growing morning irritation. So, for now, I will skip that in favour of you placing the letter to your nose.'

I lifted the letter and did as he suggested. I was about to protest when I caught a faint whiff of perfume. I smiled and he must have understood as he nodded.

'How many of your correspondences smell vaguely of a woman's perfume, Watson? None I'll warrant, no, that settles the matter.'

I placed the letter on the side and studied the postmark on the envelope. There was a faint smudging on the print, but this was the only indication visible to me. I looked up at Holmes, who handed me his glass. The print was as it should be. I was about to drop the whole thing when I saw what must have been the reason for Holmes' observation. The date was not consistent with the delivery time.

'The letter was dated nine o'clock yesterday evening, but I received it at eight o'clock that same day.' Holmes reached over and poured himself more coffee; he had consumed at least a whole pot.

'Not quite, Watson, but I appreciate your enthusiasm. Actually, I had not picked up upon that point, although it would have been difficult to do so, as I was not here when the letter arrived. No, if you look closer you will see that the town, Norwood, sits above the area postcode as usual, which may be in the correct place on the envelope, but appears to be in the wrong place geographically. Since when is Norwood in northwest London?'

I saw it at once. Holmes must have understood as his eyes fell upon the toast, but his smile indicated he saw the realisation that I now know is very readable in my face. The postmark should have been southeast London.

Holmes took the letter back and looked at the postmark again.

'There is a thumbprint which has smeared the ink slightly. My first impression was the post official might have accidentally smeared the postmark, but on reflection and through the lens I saw the alteration clearly enough.'

We both ate a full breakfast in silence. I rested upon the couch once I had finished my breakfast and picked up the morning's paper, to see if I could find any further clues in the agony columns that would help in our investigations. Holmes lit his after-breakfast pipe and began to blow huge circles of smoke into the air.

'Do you think the letter came from Lady Wilburton, then?'

Holmes shrugged. 'Or possibly from the mother. Time will tell.'

I was still working on my notes at around ten thirty, when Holmes re-entered our sitting room.

'I must go out and follow up on some leads with Mycroft. I shall meet you for lunch tomorrow at the little Italian restaurant along Oxford Street. Say, one-thirty?'

I acknowledged his request. 'You'll be out all night then?'

'With a view to wrapping as much of the case up as possible.'

'Then I'll dress your arm now, before you go.'

'Splendid.'

After I had washed and redressed his wound, Holmes made his way to his bedroom.

When thirty minutes had passed, I heard the front door close and Mrs Hudson looked up as I peered over the banister. 'Was that Mr Holmes going out?' I enquired.

Mrs Hudson shrugged her shoulders.

'Not that I recognised, Doctor.'

Mrs Hudson nodded, leaving the hallway and closing the doors to her own private sitting room.

As predicted, Holmes did not return that evening and breakfast was at least a quiet affair. At around midday I got myself ready and finally began the journey to Oxford Street. It was a busy lunchtime, with many people shopping. Gino's was full, but as always, Holmes had left nothing to chance. When I entered, the proprietor waved me in, and pointed to the only empty table in the establishment. It was reserved for me.

There was no sign of Holmes, so I ordered a coffee and waited. I observed a couple of men sitting at tables around me. Gino often gave back to the community, allowing, where others refused, the impoverished within his establishment. It was one of the many reasons Holmes and I dined there. However, on observing them, I couldn't shake the feeling these men were not typical of the types of patrons Gino would usually assist. And my mind was further made up, when he gestured furiously at them to leave. The leader made a drunken effort to dissuade the proprietor from throwing them out. After his conversation, he staggered over to my table and sat down.

'I'm sorry, but that seat is taken,' I remarked, unconsciously feeling for the trusty old service revolver I had regrettably forgotten to bring.

'You Watson?' he slurred.

He wore a patch over his left eye, was unshaven and had a scar running along the length of the left-hand side of his face, but I had been fooled too often to not see through it.

'You know very well who I am, Holmes,' I hissed.

He grinned. 'Pray act as though you don't know me. Our lives may depend on it.'

I ran my eye out the window and noticed two unsavoury characters watching from across the street.

'You noticed our watchers? You are improving.'

'Experience,' I remarked coldly. It was not an act.

'What danger are we in now?'

'The worst kind, I'm afraid.'

'How far have you got with your plans?'

He pulled out a rough-edged white box with cigarettes inside. They were of a lower class of smoke than he usually cared for, but when he got into disguise, he got completely into character right down to the smallest detail. He lit one of the foul-smelling things as he spoke.

'I don't have time to explain everything. Let's just say, I was correct about Oberstein's involvement, but he doesn't have the originals as I previously suspected. Mycroft has the government locked down in some internal investigation, to gain us time. Sir Henry had made copies but his daughter did not take them, and she never left England. You were correct about Trelean. I tracked him down last night. He's an American, Watson. A Pinkerton agent in fact, and a good one too.'

'You know more about him now?'

Holmes shook his head. 'Almost nothing.'

'Then what made you say he was good?'

Holmes smiled. 'He fooled me entirely. I would offer this as proof of his expertise. Would you not agree?'

I nodded. 'So, you were able to track him down?'

He shook his head. 'He found me. I was close to finding Lady Wilburton. It turns out he's been protecting her this entire time. The American's have a case against Sir Henry. She's their principal witness.'

'But will they give her up?'

'No. We discussed it, but the American's want Sir Henry. They want him rather badly. Mycroft and I are inclined to give him to them.'

'But he would escape justice here, were that to happen.'

He hissed at me. 'You forget he's too well protected here.'

'You're right, I did forget. But wouldn't that protection extend to America?'

'Oh no.' Holmes flashed me a toothy grin, and I was appalled by his black-and-yellow teeth.

'Well, I'm not sure I approve. What does she get out of this deal?'

'Escape from prosecution. A way out from under her father's influence. A chance at a new life. Take your pick.'

I shuddered. 'It all seems underhand and, well, very un-British.'

'You are a romantic, Watson. I can't blame you for that. Some of the world's worst dictators are products of British

Foreign Policy, and British teachings. Most of them went to Eton. But I see you disagree with me, so perhaps we can discuss this at a more appropriate time?'

He tapped his pocket. 'I have the forged documents.'

'How?'

'I bought them from Sir Henry this morning.'

I was shocked. 'You did what?'

'I went to his offices in Westminster and bought them for the handsome price of five hundred pounds. They are extremely good. The originals I thought I'd tracked to Oberstein, but he doesn't have them. And at least there is one thing we can be assured of. There will be no further complications with Oberstein.'

'How is that?'

'Because he is dead.'

'Murdered?'

'Probably.'

'You don't know?'

Holmes shrugged. 'I don't care to know.'

This was unlike Holmes. He was a champion of law, so I had to imagine he had a good reason for his callousness.

'Sir Henry had the forged documents with him, in Westminster? The guile of this man. But why would he sell them to you?'

'He had gained the impression I was a rogue agent working on behalf of a European Royal household, looking to gain a foothold in British territory.'

'How did he come to believe this?'

'It's easy, when the entire machine of Special Branch is behind you. Not to mention the Treasury.'

He smoked his cigarette, blowing the smoke across us.

I was confused and voiced it. 'But why would he sell them?'

'He's feeling the heat, I fancy. When he offered them for the price of five hundred pounds, along with certain other conditions, it occurred to me he must still have eyes on the originals. Otherwise he would have asked for more.'

I frowned. 'Five hundred pounds is a considerable amount.'

Holmes shrugged. 'The originals may be worth ten times that, if the consequences are as claimed.'

'I still don't understand what he hopes to achieve by selling off copies?'

Holmes smiled. 'He can sell as many copies as he wants, to as many idiots who try to buy them. He knows they can't use forgeries, and frankly, unless the person buying them had access to the originals, they could never know they were copies. You see? It's just another scam. But this time his greed will get the better of him. Now I must go.'

Holmes made gestures in the air, as though he was trying to sell me something. He waved his hands around a wooden box. I declined and asked him to leave. He grunted at me and dropped a paper he screwed up onto the table. With the box under his arm, he stormed off.

Chapter Eleven

Holmes returned by three o'clock the following afternoon in a different disguise, but when he entered the rooms, he threw off the disguise and made a headlong rush into his bedroom. Our afternoon tea was on the table and so I sat down and poured.

'All is working perfectly, Watson,' said Holmes as he left the bedroom.

Holmes smoked his pipe and laid out four pages on the table. 'Here are the copied documents.'

I looked them over with trepidation, for I knew the damage these could present. Holmes shoved his arms outward, like a conjurer about to pull a card out of thin air.

'And here are the originals,' he said. With a flash the documents appeared on the table.

I jumped from my chair as I looked down at the documents before me. They were cream coloured as had been described and had a purple silk ribbon around them. Holmes stood smiling at me and I must have looked foolish as I let out a very hearty laugh.

'My God, Holmes, you really have done it.' I could not contain my enthusiasm.

Holmes for his part patted me on the back and dropped himself into his favourite chair with a very wide smile.

'The case practically solved itself,' he said, matter-of-fact, although as I have mentioned on many occasions he did delight in praise for his unique and singular abilities.

'With the aid of Mycroft. We made a deal with Trelean, our Pinkerton friend.' Holmes lit his pipe.

'In exchange for assurance Sir Henry would find his way to America, he took us to Lady Wilburton, or Lady Sarah as she prefers to be called. Apparently, she has kept records of her father's schemes and although I do not believe for one instant, she is in any way free of guilt, certainly not for the deaths of all those poor suitors. She has no desire to hang. Our deal was rather loathsome, I admit, but in exchange for her support, she will be allowed to leave England to start a new life in America. The American's have already organised everything. It was she who had the documents, but not the forgeries as we suspected. She switched them on her father. I don't even think he suspects the subterfuge.'

I was full of questions, but Holmes held up a hand to me.

'You shall hear all before the night is out.'

I heard our bell ringing and watched as Holmes sprung from his chair.

'Ah, that will be our illustrious client, Lord Défarrus now.' Holmes opened the door, and our client approached us with a grave expression upon his face.

'I received your message and am here as you dictated.'

Holmes shook his hand. 'You are right on time, come in. My brother has given you a run through of events?'

He nodded. 'I'm up to speed. The audacity of it astounds me.' It was at that point His Lordship's eyes turned to our table. He took in a breath. 'You have the documents upon your table! Explain yourself, sir, for I am most anxious to know how you came about them!' Holmes stood with his pipe in hand.

'My Lord, you will hear a full account of it before the evening is up. I have some instructions. Once I have given them, I must ask you to dispatch your brougham. I will ask you to wait patiently in my bedroom. You will be rewarded for your patience.'

Holmes was very strict with his orders, and Défarrus listened carefully to all of his instructions. When Holmes finished, he left our rooms, released his brougham for the evening and re-entered, seating himself down on our settee. Holmes turned towards him and offered a cigar.

'This has been a delightful case, my Lord. I would think it might be one of my greatest, although if Watson here puts pen to paper, it could become one of my longest.'

'But you must let me in on the secret. My agents were unable to deduce anything from this affair. I tried to speak with Sir George about it but he has been curiously busy. So, am I to conclude that you have been keeping me deliberately in the dark?' His expression was one of sheer delight crossed with a slight frown. Holmes nodded as he spoke.

'You have been, and there is a very valid reason why.'

'I will defer to you then, on what must be done.'

'Thank you. I have not been without some degree of loss where this case is concerned. But hark, I hear a footstep upon our stairs. You must follow my instructions. I will give you the sign when I am ready. You fully understand? Excellent, it is settled. Take yourself a drink and be quiet!'

Holmes repositioned himself in his chair, and I sat facing the doorway. In an instant, Sir Henry Wilburton stood in our sitting room. Holmes gestured.

'Pray enter, Sir Henry.'

The man was as Holmes originally described, a face full of hatred, reddening and obese. He stared at us both and with as much dignity as he could muster, entered our rooms. He eyed me for the longest time, before finally turning to Holmes.

'I can spare you five minutes, sir, no more. I am not accustomed to being summoned by the likes of you.'

Holmes let out a humorous exclaim and I motioned for Sir Henry to enter.

'You laugh, sir, but I assure you I am a much more dangerous an adversary than you could imagine.' Holmes and Sir Henry locked eyes for the briefest of moments, but I was gratified to see it was Sir Henry who looked away.

'The game is up,' Holmes began. 'I have you and all of your men. Even now my brother and Inspector Lestrade are questioning Wilhelm on his activities in this case. I have all of your heavies and I now have you. You would do yourself more credit and serve justice by confessing this treasonous affair to Doctor Watson and myself here. It is the only escape for you now, for if you don't, I shall go public with all I know.'

Sir Henry moved towards the table and looked down at the documents. If he was concerned, he made no expression to betray it. In fact, he turned and smiled and took a seat on the settee.

'I'm sure you think you have me on some scandal or other, but I am used to such accusations. I believe this Wilhelm of whom you speak was the murderer of Lieutenant Wilson? The Dartford Police bestowed this information upon me today. Aside from the fact it happened in my house, I had nothing to do with it. And you cannot prove I did, or I would be in a police station, and not in your sitting room. Unless you wish to tell me, you have some actual evidence?'

Holmes stood with his back towards the fire, his long arm draped the mantle. Sir Henry never took his eyes off him, and I, for that matter, never took my eyes of Sir Henry.

'I will lay the facts before you. Wilhelm gave you up. He confessed you paid him to deliver certain documents to Hugo Oberstein. Wilson recognised the fullness of your crime and he also realised the documents you had belonged to the government. He suspected the treasonous plot behind your use of them,' Holmes said, pointing to the evidence laying on the table.

'Wilson confronted you about it. Wilhelm as we both know is a rogue agent and not sanction by any government.' Holmes stopped by the bedroom door and looked at his pocket watch.

'Your position in the Foreign Office and Select Committees gave you access to confidential top-secret files, including foreign agents and their handlers. Mycroft confirmed what you explained in our first interview, that leaked information to foreign agents is sometimes a sanctioned practice, but not officially. You knew where to go then, who to meet. Is Charing Cross Station still the customary meeting place? Wilhelm's services were available but not cheap. Organising Wilson's death was easy, covering it up was difficult. Someone had to put the revolver in Wilson's hands. That was Stepson. He fired off a round, leaving the empty cartridge within, and the weapon in the dead man's hand. But why did he wear your boots? I could not find a satisfactory answer until I checked the boots. In your haste to appear out of the house, when Wilhelm was laying in wait for Wilson, you put on Stepson's boots by mistake. Giving the impression that you had approached the body, when in fact you had not. Wilhelm then left with your daughter for London, whereupon he took the documents you had been copying that morning, handing them to Hugo Oberstein.'

Sir Henry nervously looked from me to Holmes.

'This is fiction. There's no evidence...'

'Patience, we will arrive there soon. Now here is where things started to go awry. Oberstein recognised the papers Wilhelm was trying to sell him, were forged and not originals. You, of course, had no idea about that. It must have been very inconvenient to discover that Wilhelm had killed Oberstein in the dispute.'

'Considering Wilhelm will probably hang for Oberstein's death, he made a full and signed confession. Another to add to my collection. Both are prepared to stand up in court and swear you were behind the affair. Sir George Stiller is being interviewed by Special Branch. I wonder what he will say to save his skin? It seems unlikely he'll remain loyal to you, a subordinate. At any rate, it is my belief you were blackmailing him, something Special Branch is already investigating.'

Holmes re-lit his pipe. Sir Henry remained calm.

'As I said before, you have no proof of anything. It's all supposition. All theories. You have been very frank with me, so let me return the favour. You say I am guilty, well, I don't deny that. But there is no one who will say a word against me. Sir George is weak. Not even he has anything on me. Shadows and whispers aren't enough, Mr Holmes. You really aren't going to get far with just those.' He wiped his sweating brow.

I noticed Holmes was like a coiled spring, rolling slowly on the balls of his feet. Sir Henry lay his hands flat in his lap.

'Your facts are precarious; you must see this? A signed confession obtained from Wilhelm, a known criminal and consult of vile foreign agencies. There can be no public interest in pitting this man against me, an honoured knight of Her Majesty's most Britannic Realm.' I could tell he was buying into his own narrative.

'Stepson is also a spurious character. I would not imagine his evidence would hold up either, since I had to remove him from service for allowing a servant to sell private family documents, to you, I am led to understand. Hopefully what you paid him will keep his son alive in the winter months. Foreign agents. Spies whose identities now revealed are left ruined and vulnerable. What other secrets does he have, hmm? How long do you think it will be before he turns up dead, after one of his own kinsmen comes to silence him? He is a far more dangerous fellow than I think you give him credit. Therefore, sir, all you have is Sir George.' He chuckled.

'So, if your case is based on the testimony of a traitor, because that's what he is … those papers you have are proof of his crimes, not mine … Please go ahead, it's fine. At any rate, and as we are being so candid, I have papers on him too, safely locked away. All the time I draw breath I am a threat to him; unless he wishes his affairs to be made public, which would of course be handled by an agent even you would find hard to trace back to me. Is this it? Is this the great Sherlock Holmes? I have to admit … I am a little disappointed.'

A smug smile crept across his rotund and overfed face. Then Holmes smiled; it was the smile I had seen so often. 'You smile, sir, but I assure you I will not be beaten. You have no way of knowing who my most loyal contacts are. So, really. What do you have, hmm?'

'I have your daughter.'

Sir Henry's smugness caught in his throat. It was the first time I had seen him falter, lost for words. But he recovered enough of his bluster to offer a tight smile.

'You have nothing. Sarah will give nothing to you.'

'She already gave me the original documents, including records of all her activities on your behalf.'

'You lie. She would never—'

'Lieutenant Wilson. You do know she loved him? She'd gone along with the other murders just fine, she was young, and she knew what she was getting into. But Wilson was different … she fell in love with him. And you had him killed.'

'No … she couldn't. I don't believe there is anything that would make her turn.'

'She's carrying his child.'

Sir Henry almost fainted. 'Impossible … am I betrayed by my own daughter?' He sighed. 'Well, no matter. I have many friends, Mr Holmes. You and your cleverness cannot outwit them all. I've weathered a scandal or two in my time, and I'll weather this one. And you, Doctor Watsit, might find it very hard to make a living having been struck from the Medical Registrar.'

I snarled, but Holmes held up a hand. 'Have you heard enough, my Lord?' Holmes asked, not taking his eye off our visitor. Sir Henry turned towards the voice, and stared in shock as Lord Défarrus said, 'Indeed, I have, Mr Holmes.'

Lord Défarrus entered the sitting room with a dangerous look on his face. Holmes moved to block the door. Sir Henry stood, his eyes darting between us. He was like a cornered animal.

'I'll see you hang for this, you villain,' he shouted at Holmes, the veins protruding from his neck.

'That pleasure must surely be mine,' Holmes remarked self-righteously.

Without warning, Sir Henry gave a bellow, and rushed Holmes, forcing him against the door. The anger of the man, his frustration at having been outmatched pushed him to the brink, and he snapped.

Holmes attempted to defend himself.

I picked up the chair and advanced towards the coward. Suddenly, Sir Henry became caught by the powerful grip of Lord Défarrus. He looked up at the towering Lord and tried to struggle, but His Lordship's look quashed any fight he might have had left.

Holmes pulled a whistle from his pocket and gave three blasts. Not long after that, as the sounds of boots clambered up our stairs, he opened the door as Inspector Lestrade and two officers entered. Lestrade and the two constables took the struggling Sir Henry to one side. One constable placed a set of handcuffs on the man, whilst Lestrade read him his rights.

'Sir Henry, it is my duty to inform you that anything which you may say will be used against you. I arrest you, sir, in the queen's name as being concerned in the death of one of Her Majesty's loyal officers, and for acts of treason against the state. Take him away, lads.'

Holmes patted Lestrade on the arm and he motioned his two constables to move Sir Henry out.

'Well, Mr Holmes, this is a queer case.' Lestrade tipped the edge of his hat and left. He must have thought of something for he had stopped and then turned at the top of the stairs.

'I almost forgot myself in the excitement. This Wilhelm fellow you had me pick up. The story he's telling me is very queer. I have it all typed up, down at the station. Will you need it?'

Holmes nodded. 'I will come down in the morning and collect them.'

'As you wish, Mr Holmes. Well, goodnight, gentlemen.'

After Lestrade had bid us a good night, he left, taking Sir Henry with him. Lord Défarrus brushed himself down and offered me a smile as I replaced our chair back at its customary place around the table.

'My Lord, these I think should be safely returned to you.' I handed Lord Montague Défarrus the documents.

'Thank you, Doctor Watson and to you also, Mr Holmes. I am ashamed and appalled by this outrage. My hope is your brother's idea will be enacted swiftly.'

'What about Sir George?' I asked.

'Rest assured, he will be dealt with. Well, once again I thank you. Her Majesty will be most pleased, and so will the Premier. I must go inform him right away.' Lord Défarrus collected his belongings, and I closed my notebook, crossing the floor and offering him my hand. He shook it, then turned to Holmes and said, 'You understand, even with all the evidence you have and my testimony, there is still the very real chance this won't make it to trial?'

Holmes had settled himself in his chair and was smoking his pipe. 'Mycroft mentioned something about it. Well, as long as the two of you take care of things, I will be satisfied. The case did present me with *some* points of interest, and at any rate, I am extremely tired. Doctor Watson will see you out. I bid you a pleasant evening.'

I followed His Lordship down through the house and out onto the steps of Baker Street.

'Your friend Mr Holmes has helped to keep this country safe. The whole of Europe owes him and yourself an immense debt of gratitude. I don't think the case could have been more professionally handled by anyone in London, given the enormity of the affair.'

The London smog had already dropped over the street and I smiled at him as he departed for his cab.

'I know,' I muttered, but he was already on his way.

When I returned, I found Holmes reading a small book. He looked up and smiled.

'A satisfactory conclusion, wouldn't you agree?'

I was not so sure. 'I'll be happier when I see that vile man at the end of a rope.'

Holmes dropped his book. 'Which will never happen.'

I looked incredulously at him. 'Because of what Lord Défarrus said? They would still, after everything we went through, look to cover this up?'

'Not entirely.' He could see I was agitated. 'It's a difficult situation. They cannot cover it up, because two police forces, Scotland Yard along with Kent County have a case of murder link to Sir Henry. But how could the government admit the other part of the affair? To publicly prosecute Sir Henry on accounts of treason would be to involve the public, scandal would still be inevitable. If the contents of the documents were so damaging, there is no way the government could allow it to get to trial.' Holmes had remarked at my outrage.

'I believe in the law. I believe in justice. Your evidence was more than complete. He'll hang and there's an end to it.'

Holmes gave me a sympathetic smile. But I didn't react. I believed in the establishment and British justice. They would ensure these scoundrels all paid for their crimes.

Epilogue

It was around three months after the scandalous affair had concluded that I read with dismay Sir Henry had somehow absconded at the commencement of his trial. When I shoved the paper in front of Holmes in disgust, he pointed to a seat.

He was sympathetic. 'My dear fellow, I told you it would never come to trial.'

'Well, what are we going to do about it?' I asked, my agitation evident.

'Nothing.' He held up a hand to quash further protest. 'Watson, I knew you would not be happy with this...'

I could not contain myself. 'You knew? In advance?'

To his credit, he remained calm and perhaps his lack of emotion on the subject reminded me I was too emotional. He eventually nodded. 'I did. It was part of the arrangement.'

'Arrangement? With whom?'

'The American government. They took him, or should I say, Mycroft arrange for him to be taken. You see there could never be a trial, I tried to tell you that. But in America, he has no friends and no potential to drag the name of her Majesty through the mud. They would not care, and those friends who may have come to his defence here, would make themselves a target over there. It is the best solution all around.'

'So that's it, he just gets away with it.'

He gave me a look. 'You honestly think American justice will be kind to him?'

He was correct. 'Well,' I muttered, 'what has he done to warrant it?'

'They have a number of reasons to want him. But the Pinkerton agency are only concerned with his links to the assassination of the American Ambassador, when he was on holiday in France last year. You remember that?'

I nodded. 'I remember you working on it, but I didn't realise you had concluded it.'

Holmes sighed. 'Not every case ends with a good result. Still, I am happy to put that to bed, along with this, and a few other cases now marked solved, from my unsolved pile. So, you see there was good from this affair and Sir Henry will never trouble us, or the public again.'

And that really was an end to it. The government seized Sir Henry's family titles, land and wealth. Sarah Wilburton, with assistance from the Foreign Office and American officials, emigrated to the United States. What wasn't reported, but Holmes divulged, was a thorough cleaning of house in Westminster. Holmes had been privately decorated for his service to the queen. Inspector Lestrade of Scotland Yard spent many weeks asking questions over the affair, of which he got no answers. Lord Défarrus retired from service shortly after the case concluded, leaving his son to carry on his work.

Sir George also retired far earlier than he had planned to. There were no real winners, as far as I saw. Sir George however kept his knighthood and pension, a point I was also disgruntled about. Wilhelm, as suggested by Holmes, turned up dead. His body was found in Knightsbridge with no obvious cause of death. No doubt his reward for double crossing whichever agency he worked for.

'It is not perhaps the most stunning of victories,' Holmes mused, not looking up from his microscope. 'The last vestiges of the Moriarty clan have been removed from the public. That is something definitely worth celebrating.'

'The entire affair is scandalous,' I remarked with a sigh.

'Perhaps. When you put pen to paper, my dear friend, you should consider that your title.'

That was the last conversation Sherlock Holmes and I had on the subject.

The case was closed.

* * * * *

Additional note, Watson, 1924.

I took Sherlock Holmes' advice and named the case A Scandalous Affair. I still remember my repugnant feeling at its conclusion. I had been privileged to be involved in a number of cases proceeding this and with each new case my disgust with high society, along with my naivety, diminished, as all things must with the passing of time. Looking back, I yearn to be that man again. He, who had not been witness to the horrors of the early twentieth century. To have not experienced the very war predicted by men like Lord Défarrus and instigated by men like Sir Henry Wilburton. And to not have been witness as the world's greatest detective was lowered into the ground, forever to remain.

Gone, never forgotten.

Mr Sherlock Holmes' skill of deduction, along with his singular gift for observation was a privilege to bear witness to for all those years. If I were to write a letter to my friend, I don't know if I could find the words to express my gratitude for simply having known him. Except to say this: Thank you, Mr Sherlock Holmes, for keeping me honest and, as you once said to me so very long ago… believe me to be, my dear fellow, very sincerely yours. John.

SHERLOCK HOLMES

The Egyptian Ring

The Egyptian Ring

Just before we took supper, I had been staring out of our window onto a dreary late winter's evening. It was the type of evening that gave my old wound aggravation, and so I found myself grateful for the warmth and comfort of a fire, and thankful Holmes wasn't in an energetic mood. For it would not be uncommon, despite the inclement weather or my protests, for him to suddenly decide we go out and around London on the hunt for some clue, which I had no desire to do. Mrs Hudson had begun her clean of our apartments early, as she was preparing to visit her sister in Scotland who had been taken ill. And in order for us to give her the freedom she needed, because a Scotswoman could be difficult when she was trifled with, I convinced Holmes to take rooms with me, at the Brabham Hotel in Upper Norwood.

After our meal, Holmes suggested we finish off by smoking a pipe or two, so we retired with drinks to the smoking lounge.

Rain beat hard against the lead lined windows, and the room's soft yellow light cast eerie shadows across our furniture. Holmes, who didn't seem at all bothered by the dreariness of the evening, sat in his usual thinking pose, with feet hunched up onto his chair. I could tell his mind was elsewhere, as he had that tell-tale vacant expression, his pipe hanging loosely in his mouth. He sighed, rather dramatically, and closed his eyes. I admit it was usual to witness swings of lucidity to depression, and that often meant he had self-prescribed some stimulant, other than his work, which was of supreme importance to him. It was also a time upon which I would keep quiet, for to attempt conversation when his moods were so volatile, would be to invite vitriol retorts, and frankly I'd become quite tired of it.

I relaxed into my chair, mesmerised by the flickering light of the fire, wondering what thoughts were passing through his great brain. Every now and then Holmes would make grunting noises. As I cast my eyes at him, his remained closed. His frown of concentration switched to occasional smile, which eventually won out, pulling at his hard-set features and softening them. From experience I knew he'd figured out the solution to either a mathematical puzzle, a cypher of some kind, or he'd found the solution to a case – and as he was engaged on no less than three, I suspected the latter.

Holmes maintained he was not a man to daydream, but as a daydreamer myself, I find I am a little disbelieving of his assertion he could control what he thinks, and his mind never wandered. Perhaps he can control his thought processes, it would certainly explain his mental acuity, and perhaps I am simply projecting my own shortcomings. An evening in a hotel where inclement weather forced us in close proximity, should his mood be difficult, was always unpleasant. This, however, was not one of those times.

Light from the fire oddly enhanced his features, subtly

changing them with the flickering of the flame. After twenty minutes or so had passed, Holmes opened his eyes and refilled his pipe.

I picked up my paper and read with some interest, that a recent excavation in Egypt had resulted in a second blow to the expedition and the British Museum. It reported an eminent archaeological Professor, Jeremy Kartz, had died under tragic and mysterious circumstances. The report also indicated the professor, who by all accounts was fit and healthy, died "suddenly and violently in an antiquities presentation", of which he was the guest of honour. Local Egyptian sources close to the dig believed the professor was victim to "a heinous ancient pharaohs' curse". Further evidence to support this theory was found in the papyrus text uncovered at a dig site he recently uncovered, detailing "death to anyone who entered the sacred burial ground". The two-thousand-year-old text had been uncharacteristically written in clear detail, telling of a "violent death to befall he who enters within".

However, there were perhaps more worldly reasons for the professor's death. And a statement from the Egyptian Antiquities Service seemed to confirm it. It read: "Professor Kartz died suddenly and violently of a massive heart trauma, not by any ancient curse, and all sane people should dismiss such inventions with contempt," said eminent French Egyptologist Gaston Maspero, the head of the service.

The British Museum released a statement saying that they were, "saddened by the news, and they too would not hold to any theories of curses, and that plausible explanations and medical science would clear the matter entirely". When asked about historical evidence regarding the health of the professor, a spokesman added, "Professor Kartz had not, to our knowledge, any such heart complaint, but due to the stresses and pressures of the dig, and the recent theft of the artefacts from the site. He'd recovered and subsequently lost. It is more probable he simply overexerted himself and died as a result".

I looked up at a chuckle, to find Holmes tapping his teeth with the bore of his pipe.

'What are you reading?'

I gave him a synopsis and he nodded. 'It's very interesting,' I finished.

He shrugged then chuckled. 'If you say so. My interests lay solely in present-day mysteries. No ancient curses need apply.'

'But you review historic crime?' I countered.

He leant forwards, a sparkle in his eyes. 'Indeed. There are patterns in everything. Even the most cunning of criminals fail to realise their activities are repeats. History is important, I grant you, but come now. What am I to do with the knowledge of two-thousand-year-old curses? Purely psychological in nature, and of no significant value to me, beyond the obvious fictional thrill that you have a flair for.'

He sat back in that way that said conversation was over. And had his mood been as I had previously described, it would have been. But he must have seen I wasn't ready to let it go, so he gesticulated with his hand. 'Tell me your conclusions then, Watson.'

I smiled. 'I've studied a few curses in my time, and in my experience, they're not all as erroneous as they seem. Certainly not all of them are classed as supernatural. Did you know that in some rare cases, a virulent disease can lay dormant on the decaying flesh of a corpse?'

He seemed almost amused. 'Really, Doctor, there is no evidence that corpses pose a risk of epidemic disease after a natural disaster. Most agents do not survive long in the body after its demise, and human remains only pose a substantial risk to health in a few special cases, such as those who are unfortunate to die from say cholera, or haemorrhagic fevers. Workers routinely handle corpses and some may risk contracting perhaps tuberculosis, or some blood-borne viruses, but only if the body was say, a few days or maybe a week deceased. Certainly nothing to induce a violent myocardial infarction as described by your article. In any event, two-thousand years would leave a cadaver devoid of anything we'd recognise as flesh.'

'I concede that, but then there's still the very real possibility of airborne disease picked up by unsuspecting archaeologists. Perhaps this death is nothing more than that?'

'Perhaps he simply died of a heart attack?'

'In conditions where hygiene is not good, I believe there may be any number of reasons why a person might die in such a way.'

'That's true. Perhaps then he was bitten by a mosquito and died of malaria, or some other tropical disease. That's much more likely than stories of curses, wouldn't you agree? In any event, as a medical man, and a highly proficient one at that, what is the likelihood of such a causal factor? Remote? Negligible, perhaps?'

'Negligible, I'd agree, but it's possible.'

'Implausible would be a better epitaph.'

'Well, possible or implausible, there's room for uncertainty.'

'It's fantasy, Watson. Like the article, like the entire Ancient Egyptian Pantheon itself. Your bias has eroded your scientific judgement. It's common amongst those who don't train their minds.'

'Meaning I'm stupid?'

His callous remarks often elicited a hot-headed response, and to his credit he shook his head.

'On the contrary, I have never thought you stupid. You have an intellect in medicine that exceeds many of your peers, and were I in need – as I have been on occasions– I assure you, I would go to no other. That being said, if we are to assume then those with untrained and unfocussed minds are stupid,' he sat back into his chair, winked, and said, 'then I am surrounded by them daily.'

I laughed, and his features momentarily disappeared through a puff of blue smoke.

'I will continue to believe there are ancient and mysterious things that happen in this world we can find no logical answer for.'

'Romance is your department, Watson. Mine is observation and deduction.'

'The cold, hard reasoner, eh?'

'As you know well.'

My friend remained quiet for some time, so I continued to read the article. I admit I was lost in its detail, and my thoughts were drifting. I found myself thinking about ancient days of mythical beings, strange rituals, and kingdoms of gods. Holmes interrupted my thoughts by speaking in an uncharacteristically soft, transfixing way.

'And it came to pass, that at midnight the Lord smote all the firstborn in the land of Egypt, from the firstborn of the pharaoh who sat on the throne unto the firstborn of the captive who was in the dungeon; and all the firstborn of cattle. And Pharaoh rose up in the night, he, and all his servants, and all the Egyptians; and there was a great cry in Egypt; for there was not a house where there was not one death.' Holmes' eyes were half closed and his pipe was thrust deep into his mouth. I admit his words sent a chill up my spine and Holmes let out a little grunt of satisfaction at my expression.

'You were moved by my words, Watson?'

'I was.' Thoughts of curses and the dead plagued my thoughts for a while longer. Holmes refilled his pipe and flashed me a grin.

'The mind is very susceptible to suggestion, Watson. You read of the curse of Osiris, or Horus, or some other fictitious entity, I paraphrase from the Bible, and there you have it. One psychologically embedded belief in curses. That is how the media use it, and why the Church manages as well as it does.'

I chuckled. 'You have me. So, the possibility of the professor being infected by some ancient illness is off the table then.'

Holmes nodded.

'If the facts did not point to another argument, then however improbable your hypothesis was, I might have been open to the possibility of a cause more natural in design. However, in this case, we can certainly rule out curses and other such matters. Our only consideration here must be one of murder.'

I laughed. 'How can you jump to that conclusion?'

'It certainly isn't as big a leap as you might think. A man in clear good health, leader of an expedition to recover artefacts of significant monetary value, who dies so swiftly after a theft is discovered, is suggestive in itself. Supplanting logical and scientific evidence with notions of curses, in an environment where superstition is rife, where murder is also common place? There's ingenuity in that. I wouldn't be surprised if there are more to add to it soon enough.'

I found myself agreeing. Even though his confident reasoning was based on limited data, it did seem a little too coincidental, and a lot more logical.

There was a knock at the door and the hotel manager, Colonel George Baccarat, came into the room carrying a large brandy bowl and smoking a Havana cigar. Dressed in a dinner suit, campaign medals attached and polished, he had a military bearing that went all the way up to his neatly trimmed heavy grey moustache, which dropped slightly at the corners. His thin grey hair swept backwards, away from haggard drawn features. He nodded to us, walked sturdily towards the mantel above the fire, and placed an arm upon it. The dining room was a private one, with three interconnecting rooms, but we were the only guests. I admit his intrusion annoyed me. Holmes was unreadable.

The colonel checked his pocket watch and harrumphed when he did so. Holmes raised an eyebrow at me. He took a large mouthful of brandy, muttering something under his breath. From my observations, it was pretty clear he had something on his mind. He was making a third check of his watch as Holmes spoke up.

'Are you expecting someone, Colonel?'

He turned. 'What? No.'

'Then I can only conclude you're either unhappy by the passage of time, or that you wish to consult me, before a certain time has passed?'

The colonel's cheek twitched, which could have been his

way of smiling; it was difficult to read. When he spoke his words were hard. 'Why should you assume that, Mr Holmes?'

'Observation is a specialty of mine, Colonel,' said Holmes, matter-of-fact. 'You don't strike me as a nervous or frivolous man. And there are many other rooms whereby you may review a pocket watch in private. So, come now, how may I be of service?'

The old soldier's demeanour softened. 'Quite right, quite right, Mr Holmes. I should just come clean and get the whole damn business out in the open.' He sunk into a chair next to us and took a large drink from his brandy glass. He glanced nervously in my direction. I'd read this expression many times before, when Holmes had visitors in our rooms, and stood to leave. Holmes held up a hand and smiled.

'Doctor Watson is my colleague and partner, upon whom you can be sure of complete discretion. Now,' he said softly, 'tell us what it is that troubles you enough to check your pocket watch every minute?'

The colonel relaxed and pulled out a large neatly folded white cloth. Without further word, he handed it to Holmes, who unfolded it upon his knee. Inside was an Egyptian Ankh – a cross with a handle – stunningly beautiful and crafted in gold. It was around half an inch in depth and at least six inches in length. Carved into it were Egyptian figures and ancient hieroglyphics. Holmes lifted the golden cross and studied it in the light of a nearby lamp. He looked at me.

'I don't believe in coincidences, Watson. Look at this.' He handed me the artefact.

Considering our previous conversation, I was more intrigued than ever.

Colonel Baccarat seemed confused by our banter. I handed it back to Holmes.

'That was what started it all,' remarked the colonel as Holmes turned the Ankh over.

'I assume this originally came from Egypt?' Holmes handed it back.

'It came from a tomb in Karnak. You may have read

something about recent discoveries in the Times? There's been a lot of attention on it, especially Professor Kartz, God rest his soul.'

Holmes and I nodded.

'It's estimated to be from around the 13th or 14th Dynasty, but there's been no formal corroboration yet. This Ankh was part of the seal on an inner tomb, broken when it was removed. It is this that causes me distress, and the reason I ... I turn to you for your wisdom and advice.'

'You're welcome to both.'

The colonel wrapped the artefact back in the cloth, as if to hide it from view. That action seemed to comfort him and he finished his brandy before continuing.

'Has this got something to do with the professor's death, Colonel?' I asked.

He sighed. 'I fear so.'

Holmes said, 'Why don't you tell your story from the beginning.'

'Very well. Three months ago, I was approached by two men from the British Museum. I am a collector of artefacts, and have financed a few digs of my own. These men, Campbell and Archright, two Egyptologists, believed they had located a new undiscovered and potentially untouched tomb from the Ancient Egyptian New Kingdom of the 14th Dynasty. Professor Kartz, they explained, had validated their claims, but in order for them to proceed, they would need finance for their project, and I had been suggested in a list with a few others. I looked over their plans carefully but made no firm agreements with either. I had their credentials checked with a Doctor Chaplin at the British Museum, and with a Professor Smythe at the Egyptian Antiquities Department. Everything checked out. After some to-and-fro, I admit I was keen to learn more, so at their suggestion, I travelled to Egypt and met up with the two of them.'

Holmes asked, 'Who gave you these references?'

'Archright supplied the names to me, but I have dealt with the museum on a number of occasions and have my own contacts, so I did not rely solely on them.'

'Wise. Continue.'

'When I arrived in Egypt, we met in Cairo. Campbell and Archright came to my hotel the next morning, and we began discussing financial arrangements. I, of course, wanted to set off immediately to see the site, but they weren't eager. They were concerned my lack of experience and understanding could lead me to disturbing their work, or worse, inadvertently destroying ancient artefacts in my ignorance. There were also security issues.'

Holmes looked up. 'Such as?'

'There had been a number of thefts from other sites. Evidently, the location of the dig site sat squarely in a region disputed by two factions of some rival tribes. A number of armed conflicts had occurred, and foreigners seem to be their target.'

Holmes nodded. 'I see, pray continue.'

'Not wanting to put myself in danger, I therefore asked them for some evidence of the return on my investment. Well, they showed me some of the artefacts discovered. I can tell you, Mr Holmes, to a layman such as myself, these things seemed to me to be broken bits of old pottery, but to them it was as if they were precious jewels. In any event, I was convinced these two gentlemen were honest and hardworking and so I agreed to their funding request, so long as I had something in return, by way of investment, you understand. They both assured me when the tomb was excavated, I would be an extremely rich man and also the named benefactor of the expedition that helped discover it, meaning my name would be remembered in history alongside theirs. Happy and content, I therefore deposited the sum of five-hundred pounds into their account.'

Holmes and I both looked at each other wide eyed. The colonel stood, crossed the room to the drinks cabinet, poured himself a generous supply of brandy and settled himself back into the chair. Holmes sat with interest and I made the notes for what seemed to be an interesting case.

'Well, a month passed and I received a letter telling me victory was at hand. They had discovered the entrance to a tomb and the seal of some pharaoh who had died in the 14th Dynasty, the period they'd correctly identified from the artefacts previously discovered. As you can imagine, Mr Holmes, I was extremely happy for them both, and not a little unexcited at the prospect of being further enriched and having my name in print around the world. They furthermore asked for additional monetary supplements, as the costs had exceeded their initial expectations due to the rather large Egyptian staff, and the licenses required to further excavate the area. I sent a wire congratulating them on their discovery, and deposited a further one-hundred pounds into their account. I heard nothing for weeks and when a month had passed, I wired them asking them for a progress report. Two days later, I received a letter explaining they'd excavated the tomb entrance from the rock. I would be called upon in due time to perform an official opening ceremony as the benefactor. Three weeks went by and I received, again through the post, a letter explaining the tomb was almost ready. I would receive instructions for the opening four weeks later. That was three weeks ago.'

Holmes had absorbed the information as he listened. When the story stopped, he opened his eyes.

'Interesting, Colonel, however, I believe there is still more. Pray continue, every detail is essential.'

The colonel took a large gulp of brandy. It seemed to steady him. I offered him a box of matches and he lit his cigar, which had died in the tray.

'Thank you, Doctor,' he said and blew out the match. 'This is where the story gets … chilling.'

'An interesting choice of words.' Holmes rubbed at his chin.

'After receiving the letter, I found myself so excited I simply couldn't wait any longer. I took a boat and after five rough days, I landed in Cairo. I travelled to the Antiquities Department and showed them the letters from my associates, asking for the precise location of the excavation and a driver to take me there, so I may surprise them and watch as they unfold the sands of time. I was shown into a waiting room, whereupon an English gentleman came in and told me there was no such excavation, that any such dig would need permits from the Antiquities Department and the British Museum. No such permission had been sought or given. I laughed because they had clearly made a mistake. I handed them copies of the permits I had, but they sympathetically explained they were fake, and remained firm no permits had been issued.

'You can imagine my reaction, Mr Holmes. Utter disbelief, followed by horror, and shame. The custodian of the Antiquities Department suggested I had been the victim of an elaborate extortion. I visited Professor Kartz at his dig site, and went through the entire thing with him. He was very understanding, and promised to make full enquiries, but he'd never heard of them either and worse, had not validated any artefacts other than his own. He told me of the troubles he'd had with thefts and so on. It seems to me he was indicating the Antiquities Department had something to do with it, and when I questioned him, he just changed the subject.

'I took the next boat back to England and visited the British Museum. When I asked to see Doctor Chaplin again, I was astounded to find no such person worked for the museum and no records of either Campbell or Archright existed. Which is ludicrous, and I admit my annoyance got the better of me.'

Holmes pondered on his thoughts for a few seconds. 'Interesting, Colonel, very interesting. What of your own contact? You said they had validated these men.'

'Doctor Barns? Well, he's vanished.'

Holmes frowned annoyance. 'Into thin air? Please, Colonel, explain.'

'He failed to report to work some weeks previous. They reported him missing. I fear the worst.'

'I see.' Holmes was thoughtful.

'It is possible Barns was in on the whole thing,' I voiced.

'Agreed,' Holmes said. 'Or worse, he's been silenced.'

'Whatever the outcome,' the colonel said with a sigh, 'he's not around to explain himself, and that's a problem. He was the only evidence I had these men existed.'

Holmes looked at the fire. 'Convenient,' he said. Then he turned back to the colonel. 'What did you do next?'

'Well, what could I have done? I left it there, licked my wounds and rethought my generosity for the future, and that would have been the end of it, except upon returning home, I found two things amiss. First, my room in the hotel had been burgled with nothing of value taken, and on that same morning, I received another letter, telling me the final arrangements were made for my visit, and I was to wait until I received word from them. They were emphatic that I should, under no circumstances, travel to Egypt alone. Somebody would come and collect me. You see now why I am confounded by this mystery.'

Holmes lit his pipe again. 'Did you respond to this letter?'

'No, I did nothing.'

'Excellent. Have you had the Ankh examined?'

'Yes, by an associate of mine who is an amateur archaeologist. He believed it to be genuine. It's certainly real gold.'

'As I suspected. Did your associate give you a true value?'

'He suggested the scrap value alone, based on the weight and the current value of gold, would fetch five-thousand pounds. It would most definitely be more valuable in its original form. You see now why I am perplexed?' The colonel shook his head glumly.

'And since Professor Kartz has now died, rather unexpectedly, we can assume no such enquiries were followed up?'

'I fear that to be so, yes.'

'Yet, given the value of the artefact, it seems unlikely extortion is the goal of these two men,' I remarked.

The colonel sighed. 'I reluctantly agree. But what does it all mean, Mr Holmes?'

Holmes ran the bore of his pipe over his lips. 'I would not

jump to conclusions regarding the motives of these men. Based on your own evidence, Colonel, you have been deceived in a particular and remarkable way. Firstly, their expedition is not registered with the British Museum, nor do the Egyptian authorities within the Antiquities Department know of them. That is significant, don't you think? These two men are on the verge of the greatest discovery since the tomb of Ramesses II and no one has heard of them? Secondly, there is the curious incident of the wire.'

'But I received no wire,' remarked the confused colonel.

'That is the curious incident, Colonel. Did the letters received by you mention in any small way the content of the telegrams you sent them?'

'No, they didn't. Good god! I hadn't even thought of that.'

'It is possible they were unaware of your own communication. No, it's far more likely each letter had been written in advance. Being sent at prearranged times. The fact you received them after you sent a telegraph was purely by chance. Why would they not communicate their response via that same method? They choose to post a response costly and far less efficient. That gives this case a far more calculating edge and turns it from the more commonplace crime to an inexplicable one. Extortion would seem to me to be a very good working hypothesis, and there are more players than just these two front men.'

'I would agree with you, if it weren't for this damn Ankh. Why send me an artefact worth eight times as much as the money I supplied?'

Holmes pondered for a second or so. 'Yes, that is a puzzle.' He remained in thought. The colonel watched the flames flicker in the fire.

Eventually Holmes smiled. 'I have a theory.'

The colonel looked pleased. 'Share it.'

'You must first look at the facts that build up this case. Once you establish the reality, all of the little curiosities themselves will point towards a truth. Let us then work with the hypothesis that extortion is the key. You supplied both men with five-hundred pounds, and a further one-hundred a month later. Shortly thereafter, approximately three weeks, the artefact was sent to you. You visit Egypt and discover these men do not appear to exist, and when you arrive at home, you receive a letter telling you all is ready for your arrival and you would be called for. That is an act of extreme importance. Why have somebody call for you at all. You are quite capable of travelling to Egypt under your own steam, as you have indeed done. When I heard that, I immediately suspected another motive. Your golden treasure is the key to this mystery. Of that you can be sure.'

'What should I do then, Mr Holmes?'

Holmes tapped out his pipe.

'Firstly, we are dealing with two clever and dangerous men.' Holmes thought for a moment. 'Did you keep the envelopes of the letters you received?'

The colonel pulled out a collection of papers from his jacket, and handed it to him.

'Capitol!' Holmes rubbed his hands together.

'This was the last letter I received.'

Holmes pulled out his glass and ran it over the postal mark and then took out the letter. He read it and then held it up to the light. Having watched him examine letters previously, I knew he was looking at many things. Paper quality, weight, manufacturer, the ink used, the handwriting, and of course, the postmark. He gave a shout and then settled himself in his chair.

'This is a very important piece of evidence. The paper is a far higher quality than I would have expected, but common in to most hotels, perhaps not so much outside of Europe. The ink is typical one penny bottle variety violet, not common in Egypt, although there is nothing to suggest it wasn't taken there. I can tell you this letter has not passed through the Egyptian postal service. In fact, there is no evidence this letter travelled through Egypt at all. But it has been through the sorting offices of this country, and it did originate abroad. You see, all post from abroad is further stamped. You can see here the original postmark. Do you notice alterations?'

The colonel took it and shook his head, he handed it to me but I saw nothing obvious either and passed it back to Holmes.

'It is perhaps only obvious to me then. I suspect you don't receive a lot of mail from Egypt, you wouldn't necessarily notice the forgery, but they couldn't be sure of that. This envelope concludes my thoughts upon the entire matter.'

The colonel was wide eyed. 'The scoundrels were never in Egypt at all. What is it they want from me, then? And what's so important about the envelope?' he asked, confused and angry.

'They only travelled to Egypt once and then only to maintain the pretence. Furthermore, and in order to enlist your rather unwitting services as an unsuspected contraband safe house, they showed you artefacts to convince you of their authenticity, which were no doubt just broken pottery as you originally suggested. The reason they were unhappy at your viewing of the dig site was, as you later found out, simply because there was no dig site, at least not one they had personally excavated.'

Holmes made a steeple with his fingers and crossed his legs. 'To answer your first question, they want the Ankh, Colonel. It was sent to you for safekeeping. They know its value as well as you do. They certainly didn't dig it up; although, I have no doubt at some point it was uncovered in an ancient tomb, but not by these men. The envelope's singularly important aspect is this; underneath the forged postal stamps is another, just visible with my lens. You may not see it, but I can tell you, it originated in the United States of America.' Holmes replaced the letter inside the envelope, and handed it back.

'As Doctor Watson will tell you, I do not purport to have any knowledge of Ancient Egypt or its remarkable artefacts, nor do I wish too, but what I do have is a knowledge of inventory. Specifically of the systems used to identify valuable artefacts, should they be stolen. On studying the Ankh, I observed a small but non-the-less curious scratch mark on the reverse side of the stem. It's very small, and to the untrained eye may seem to be either part of the design or from wear. But I know it as a peculiar identification system used in the New York Museum of Antiquities. I would not be surprised to learn of its theft in the fullness of time. You remarked you had been burgled yet nothing was taken. I would surmise your friends decided to visit, to collect their artefact, but upon finding you away from home, searched your room. After a fruitless search, they concluded you either stored it in a safety box, or you were carrying it on your person. In any event, that was the reason why you were to be given instructions on when you would be called for. No doubt a cab would be dispatched to collect you. One thing is for certain, had you not consulted me, you wouldn't have made it to Egypt at all.

'These calculating men both knew in order to gain the artefact they needed you in person. It was obvious they couldn't just turn up and demand it, because they had to maintain the pretence of their Egypt escapade for as long as possible.'

The colonel seemed astounded by my friend's remarkable observations.

'And I would have unquestionably gone with them too, probably to a shallow grave. What then must I do?' The colonel was excited at the prospect of resolving this affair.

'They won't wait long. The theft will hit the national press soon enough. They'll need to retrieve their trophy, and then melt it down. That way it's simply a bar of gold and can be sold anywhere. I suggest you telephone the local constabulary and have an inspector here for the morning. Your friends are sure to call tomorrow. At least you'll have a surprise waiting for them, instead of the other way around.'

Colonel Baccarat shook Holmes by the hand, nodded to me, and thanked us both. He left to put Holmes' suggestions into actions.

'There is one thing that puzzles me, Holmes,' I said to his summing up.

'What is it, Watson?'

'The money. Why did they need more?'

'Well, Watson, there you take me to the realm of supposition. Greed? Very possible. Certainly we already established extortion was their game. Even with the limited data, I'm willing to wager it was greed.'

'I suspect you're correct.'

'Do you have an answer of your own?'

'I think I do?'

'Share it with me.'

'First-class travel to New York and back is expensive.'

Holmes clapped his hands and laughed. 'I think you have it right. We shall go with your theory. But in any event, this is the tip of the iceberg. Mark my words, Watson.'

'Why do you say that?'

Holmes smiled. 'Because of Professor Kartz's death.'

'You think they're connected?'

'You think they aren't?'

I awoke the next morning to the sound of a police whistle. Holmes was already out of our rooms, and I struggled to get down in time to witness the action. Holmes and the colonel stood triumphant upon the stairs. A glint in Holmes' eye told me the case was concluded.

'Capitol, Watson, you arrive in time for breakfast.'

'Have I missed the excitement, then?' I was disappointed.

'Nothing really to report, Doctor. The scoundrels have been caught, and I'm on my way to give a statement.'

Colonel Baccarat nodded to us both as he left.

'It seems the eminent Inspector Lestrade was already on the case. When our friend here made the call last night, he came down immediately,' Holmes said as we made our way towards the breakfast room.

'I talked with Lestrade at length, and once I'd explained the situation, he filled in the missing gaps. They're calling it the Egyptian Ring.'

'Well, it's fitting,' I remarked.

'Somewhat sensational for my tastes. As you know, I suspected but couldn't be sure of a wider conspiracy. Lestrade has what he calls the ringleaders in custody. Messers Campbell and Archright are more formally known as Dawson and Powsey. Two men I have crossed paths with before. Two extremely violent men by all accounts. Colonel Baccarat doesn't know how lucky his escape was.'

'Indeed. What about the artefact?'

'Well, as New York is five hours behind us, we'll have to wait 'til they answer the wire sent, but Lestrade says the reward money is substantial. It should go some way to replacing what the colonel lost. He also took care of our bill.'

'Very generous of him.'

'Well, considering we saved his life, I should say that was the least he could do.'

'So, it's all neatly tied up, then?

Holmes said nothing as we filled our plates with our breakfasts. When we sat down, he began eating with gusto. I knew his silence meant more, so I pressed him.

'You don't believe this is the end of the matter, do you?'

Holmes chuckled in that peculiar way. 'The faculty for deductive reasoning is clearly catching this morning.'

'Well, surely the colonel's situation is explained and answered?' I asked, frowning my confusion.

'Yes, that much is true.'

'We caught our fish and Lestrade has his trophy. It's over, then?'

Between mouthfuls of scrambled eggs, Holmes smiled. 'I'm not interested in pilot fish, Watson. That's a job for Lestrade and his lackeys. There's a shark behind this entire affair. No, the game isn't over. In fact, I'd go so far as to say the game is positively afoot.'

DR. CHANDRIX DIES

BONUS
FIRST 3 CHAPTERS

PROLOGUE

London, 1930
Harley Street: Tuesday, 3rd June - 3pm

Colonel Davidson paused outside the Harley Street door of Doctor Chandrix's office to reread the letter from the previous day's post which had brought him there. The Colonel was a tall, well-dressed, clean-shaven, immaculate officer of around fifty. Retired from service, he wore his suit like a uniform. He had a slight, wiry frame, and took good care to maintain it. Taking a deep breath, he finished the cigarette he'd been smoking and without further thought, plunged through the door leading to the outer office. His abrupt entrance caused a plain young woman to look up from her typewriter. She gave him an inquiring glance.

'Doctor Chandrix,' said Colonel Davidson.

'Do you have an appointment?'

He held up the letter.

She nodded in comprehension.

'Come this way, please.'

He followed her into an inner office—into the presence of the tanned Doctor Chandrix.

'Good afternoon,' said Doctor Chandrix. 'Sit down, won't you? I expected you an hour ago.' His voice was light, but Colonel Davidson found the undertone hard to ignore. It irritated him, but he chose to swallow it.

'My name is Davidson—' he began.

'I know who you are, Mr Davidson,' said Chandrix.

'Colonel.'

'Yes, of course, Colonel. I understand you've just returned from abroad?'

'India.'

'A fine country. I have spent many years in India myself. That's how I came to know about you, if you get my meaning.' Chandrix looked over the top of his gold-rimmed spectacles. He smiled through his penetrating green eyes; they locked with Davidson's grey eyes—neither man blinked for the longest time.

Colonel Davidson used the time to examine the man. The face was lined, but the years had been good to him. His tan, though light, was darker than one would expect from the climate of England. At one time it may have been darker; his admission of having spent years in India suggested as much. The greying at his temples feathered into the darker hair above. It had been obvious from the letter that Chandrix had discovered some secret. Davidson was very interested in what that might be, but was determined to give nothing away. Conscious that this battle of wills would not get him any further, he gave ground and blinked. The doctor smiled.

'What is it you think you know, Chandrix?'

Doctor Chandrix steepled his fingers and tapped at his lips as he considered the question. He opened his hands and placed them on the table. Eye contact was never broken. He made an imperceptible movement with his brow and with slow undertaking, pulled a bundle of letters tied with a silk ribbon from the inside pocket of his jacket. Colonel Davidson's eyes narrowed.

'You do recognise these, don't you, Colonel?' The provocative way he waved them made the Colonel's eye twitch.

'Looks like random correspondence to me,' Davidson replied.

'Tut... tut... Colonel. That's not becoming of an officer.

Certainly not one of your standing, experience, and reputation.'

Davidson said nothing.

'Let's not start this conversation with bluff,' he cautioned.

'Well, I can't see them from here.'

'Yet you can recognise them.' Chandrix flicked through the handful of papers, gauging the colonel's reaction.

He was not disappointed.

Davidson's eventual sigh was an admission.

'Yes, yes. I know what they are. The question is, how do I get them back?'

Chandrix's face seemed etched in a permanent smile. He leant forward a little.

'An excellent question, Colonel, really excellent,' a momentary pause then, 'but I have a better one.'

'Oh? How much, I suppose. It's all about money with your type, isn't it?'

'Please, Colonel!' Chandrix sounded disgusted. 'This was never about money.'

Davidson could discern no deceit. 'What then?'

'It's very simple. What would you do to get them back?'

'If you've read them, and I assume you have—and if you've spent the time in India you say you have—you know the answer to that.'

Nodding, Chandrix said: 'Then I'm sure we can come to an acceptable arrangement?'

Colonel Davidson gave a slight tilt to his head. 'You seem very sure of yourself.'

Doctor Chandrix returned the letters to his pocket. He opened a drawer in his desk and pulled out a bottle of single malt and two glasses. After pouring the whiskey, he lifted his glass.

'To our future arrangements?'

Colonel Davidson reached for his glass. Without breaking eye-contact, he passed it under his nose. He paused to savour the contents, tilted his head back and then downed it in one gulp.

'What stops me putting a bullet in your head and just taking them?' He placed the glass on the table and Chandrix poured him another.

'Nothing. Nothing at all.'

Colonel Davidson took the refilled glass and considered his next move.

'You're a very brave man, Doctor.'

Chandrix smiled.

An hour later, the Colonel entered a telephone box and closed the door. Pulling out a handkerchief, he picked up the receiver and dialled. He watched as a couple with a pram ambled along the road. They were absorbed in their conversation and paid him no attention.

A voice answered.

Davidson spoke: 'George? Good. Listen—no, listen—it's on. What? No, forget that. He's taken the bait. Yes, I have what we need. Are you sure? I... no... It's fine. Yes, yes, of course. I'll go there right away. When? Well, that's up to you, George. I have to go.' He put down the receiver, wiped it with the handkerchief and walked out onto the street. Satisfied no one had observed him, he walked away with a casual stride. As he passed the couple with the pram, he lifted his hat. He turned and crossed the street, disappearing down an alley.

On the opposite side, in the shadow of another side street, a man in a dark suit and overcoat, hat pulled down so only his chin was visible, flicked the cigarette he had been smoking onto the road.

He watched the couple pushing the pram approach. As they passed, a male voice said, 'It's him.'

He pulled up his collar and crossed the road...

Chapter One

Brighton
The Royal Albion Hotel: 4th June - 3pm

Doctor Pieter Straay sipped his beer as he flipped through the
Times. A shadow passed over him and instinct made him look
up.

'Doctor Straay?' the young lady asked, shielding her eyes
from the sun. 'I knew it was you. Do you remember me? Mary.
Mary Davidson.'

'Mary?' Straay stood and took a better look at her. Mary
Davidson. It was ten years since he'd last seen her. The changes
in her were considerable.

Straay had always been fond of Mary as a child. Because of
his friendship with Colonel and Mrs Davidson, they had spent
a significant amount of time together until Mary's mother
became ill. When that happened, the Colonel took his wife left
Holland, and travelled back to England and Mary had been
packed off to India to spend time with her uncle. She had lived
a good many years with him before returning to England
herself. Although Straay and Mary hadn't laid eyes on each
other for most of that time, they had been in regular contact.
For the last few years, however, this contact had been broken.

'You don't recognise me, do you?' She pouted a little.

'Of course I remember you, Mary.'

She embraced him. If she noticed how awkward he found

it, she said nothing.

'Oh how marvellous,' she beamed. 'May I join you?'

He gestured at the chair.

'I was standing over there,' she indicated, 'when I thought, I must come over and say something, but I wasn't sure if you'd recognise me! How long have you been in England?'

'About a week.' Straay smiled at her. Mary had grown into an attractive young woman in her twenties. Her smart business-like dress seemed out of place for a seaside resort.

'Do you work here?'

She raised an enquiring eyebrow. The question appeared to annoy her. 'Why do you ask?'

He shrugged. 'You don't seem, if you'll pardon my saying, dressed for vacation.'

She looked forlorn at the sea, and sighed.

'You're right. I wish I was on vacation.' Mary turned back to him and relaxed. 'I just started working for a doctor here as his receptionist, nurse, and general dogsbody.' She laughed, but without humour. There was something unreadable behind her blue eyes. Straay kept his expression neutral as he continued to study her. 'It's not a bad job, you know, as jobs go. I don't mind it. He pays well, but I don't get a lot of time off.'

'How is your father?'

'He's well, thank you. I haven't seen much of him of late. He was posted to India for some hush-hush mission, so I decided to move down here.' She gestured to the waiter who approached the table. After ordering a pink-gin she turned back to Straay. He folded his paper and placed it on the table. He picked up his beer and took another swallow. She tugged anxiously at her earlobe and when the waiter arrived with her drink, she ordered another. She then took a large gulp. It seemed to steady her.

'You miss your father?'

'Very much. I wish I hadn't been so stubborn. I could have gone with him, you know.'

'Do you correspond?'

Her second drink arrived. Straay shook his head at the

offer of a refill.

'Once or twice a month. Do you?' She sipped her second drink.

'I keep in contact.' He lifted his beer to his lips and then paused. 'Have you seen much of your mother?'

She looked down for a moment. 'I can't.'

He put down the glass. 'You can't? Or you won't?'

'I just don't have the time to go to London. I'm too busy. Besides… Mother doesn't know who anyone is anymore. The last time I went, she wouldn't believe I was her daughter, so… I can't. It's too hard.'

Straay understood. 'So you work here for this local doctor. He gives you the fatherly advice you miss?'

'I'd much rather have your advice,' she teased. 'You were always unorthodox, as I recall. There were plenty of times your advice landed me in hot water, but it always seemed right.'

Straay laughed.

Mary became serious. 'I do want to talk to you, though.'

'Is everything all right?'

She finished her drink. 'I dare say I'm a fool,' she said, 'but I think there's something wrong.'

There was a moment's silence. She felt awkward under Doctor Straay's intense gaze.

'Something wrong? How?' His sharp question startled her.

'I don't know… That's what I wanted your help with. But I've felt—more and more—there is something not quite right. I saw you arrive at the hotel yesterday; that was when I decided to put the entire thing before you and, well, enlist your help, to—oh, I don't know—somehow advise me. I know I'm being very vague… Call me silly if you like, but I think if there was news of a murder, here, tomorrow, I shouldn't be surprised by it!'

Doctor Straay stared at her. She looked back with youthful defiance.

'That's very interesting,' he remarked.

'I suppose you think me a complete idiot.'

'I have never thought of you as an idiot, Mary,' he said with a smile.

'I don't have anything to support it. It's just a feeling—intuition. Nothing at all tangible.'

'Don't dismiss intuition, Mary. You may have noticed something or heard something you can't define. Considering your father's occupation, it would be normal for you to see more than the average person. It is not foolishness, Mary, for someone to not know why they are uneasy.'

Mary seemed relieved. 'That's it exactly. I don't know what it is—I just have this feeling there may be a murder. Well, someone might die at any rate.'

'Tomorrow?'

'Maybe, or perhaps the next day.'

'You don't have any idea who?'

'No. And if I did I'd go to the police!' She sighed and rubbed her temple.

'What has happened to arouse this feeling?'

'It's all got to do with the practice. Doctor Chandrix—'

'Chandrix? He's the doctor you work for?'

'Yes, Brian Chandrix. He's the son of Doctor—'

'Simon Chandrix, of Harley Street. Yes, I know him.' Straay frowned.

'Oh, yes, I should have realised, you being in the same profession and all that.'

He reached over and took her hand. The movement startled her.

'Tell me what it is that has worried you so.'

'Well it's a mixture of things, really: overheard conversations, half-glimpsed looks, certain patients who have fallen ill, and yet...these people are old and it's expected they might, you know, die. Take Mrs Leigh: she's eighty and fit as a flea! Last week she was found dead—the doctor says it was due to natural causes, she was old... I can't speak as a doctor, but I saw her records. Her heart was that of a woman twenty years younger. She wasn't on any drugs; she didn't smoke, didn't drink.

'Police weren't interested...no reason to be. There wasn't

even an investigation. What if someone had murdered her, though? Like I say, it's nothing tangible because people do just drop dead at eighty; that's very old!' She sighed. 'But I did some checking, and do you know there have been a lot of older people dying here—people who were fine...then, well, they're dead.

'Then there are the ones who leave all their money to some big club in London—you know the type. People you didn't even know had any money. Nine times out of ten, they leave it to the local cat and dog home.'

'It is a convalescent resort, Mary. Lots of retirees. The rate of death will always be higher in an elderly community.'

She nodded. 'I know, but what if someone was killing them off? It is possible.'

'I begin to understand,' he said. 'You permit me to speak with your father?'

'I can't stop you, but why?'

'Because I want you to join him.' He withdrew his hand.

'How could I?' She looked uncertain.

'Leave the details to me. If I arrange it, you'll go?'

'What about my job? What about my life here? I can't just walk away from everything.'

'Do you have many friends here?'

'Well no, but –'

'A boyfriend?'

She blushed.

'Your employer?'

'Well... it's nothing serious,' she evaded.

'But it is something?'

'Something, yes.' She nodded.

He was dead serious.

'Is there anything else, apart from your job and the something you have with Chandrix, you could not walk away from?'

'No.' She sighed, but there was light behind her eyes, which hadn't been there before. It gave him hope.

'You'll go then, if I arrange it?' he asked again.

She bit her lip while she thought. Her mind made up, she nodded.

'Good, then go pack your things. I will come to your home. Please write down the address on my pad.'

She complied.

'Go, I will join you later. Say nothing to anyone.'

Doctor Straay watched as Mary made her way through the crowd. He opened the pad and for the longest time he studied her address. Satisfied, he closed it and pulled an envelope from inside his jacket. He read the letter it contained. With care he put it back in his pocket, and turned his eyes to the sea. Pulling out a pen, he made a note on the margin of his newspaper.

Chandrix was a name he hadn't heard for some time. And now, today, he'd heard it...twice. It couldn't be a coincidence. Mary was in danger, and at least he could get her to safety. He tapped his pen on his notepad in thought. His mind made up, he closed the pad and grabbed his newspaper. It hadn't, of course, been a coincidence that he'd chosen to come to England. Mary had been the reason. He'd searched for her for some time. Now she had found him. When he'd first started out on the quest, he hadn't considered Mary would be in any real danger. She was capable, resourceful, and careful. Now, however, things had changed. Mary had embroiled herself in a situation she didn't understand; a situation that might very well harm her. He couldn't tell her, at least not right away, that he and her father were working on the Chandrix case—Simon Chandrix.

He was about to return to the hotel when a waiter slipped in beside him.

'Excuse me, sir, but if you've finished with your copy of the Times, I'd really enjoy reading it.'

'By all means.' He handed the paper to him. 'The classified section is very interesting. I would pay particular attention to it.'

Mary reached her apartment and followed Doctor Straay's instructions. She didn't have many clothes or possessions; she'd learnt to travel light over the years. She packed her bag and tidied her room. Satisfied, she lit a cigarette, picked up a newspaper, and sat in the chair by her bed. The headline had a sensational title: "Suicide in the Thames". Absorbed, she didn't hear the door open. A flicker of movement caught her eye and she looked up, the colour draining from her face.

'Hello, Mary,' a male figure said.

Chapter Two

Brighton
The Royal Albion Hotel: 4th June - 4pm

The lobby of the Royal Albion was luxurious. The lavish décor impressed all who visited. The hotel itself was the hub of all activity in Brighton. Recent bad press notwithstanding, the clientele were there to enjoy their summer holidays free of real world difficulties. A mixture of young and old, in political or theatrical professions, mingled in its bars, on the tennis courts, and in its three dining rooms. It really was the place to be.

Doctor Straay lifted the receiver in the hotel lobby and started to dial. Before he could finish, a gloved hand pushed the cradle down. He turned to see a red-faced man in a pin-striped suit, his right hand covered by an overcoat, pointing at him. He looked almost apologetic.

'I wonder if we could just take a minute of your time before you make that call, Doctor Straay,' he said. His eyes moved towards a second man.

Straay replaced the receiver with care. The other man approached—much older, with silver-white hair, dressed almost the same and supported by a silver-handled black cane. He bowed as he approached. Here is a man who's in the services. Old enough to be in a commanding position, Straay mused. His limp still causes him pain; his face contorts with each step he takes. But it's not a recent injury; the cane is well used. Its tip has worn away to the harder metal beneath. He turned to the red-faced man. Both wear similar suits, almost regulation. The regulation way they dress suggests they aren't criminals. They must therefore be officials. But not police—how interesting.

The elder stranger put both hands on his cane and raised himself to full height. At just under six feet, he wasn't quite as tall as Straay, but he gave the impression of being taller. 'I realise this is rather unorthodox, Doctor, but I must insist you follow me.'

Straay remained silent. He had the feeling he knew this man. He followed him but kept the other within his peripheral vision. He was led into a small conference room. Red-face stood by the door. Silver-hair handed him his cane, then sat and indicated a chair.

'Won't you sit, Doctor, please?'

'MI5?' Straay asked. The other raised an eyebrow.

'Doctor,' he said, 'sit.'

Straay sat, he studied the face. There was something familiar in it, and he knew he'd met this man before, many years ago. For the moment, he couldn't recall the name.

The elder man removed his gloves and indicated the start of business by crossing his legs.

Straay pulled out his cigarette case and lifted it.

'Oh by all means, Doctor. Smoke away.'

Straay lit a cigarette and blew out the match with the smoke. Silver-hair finished folding his gloves and made himself comfortable. 'Ah... there we are.'

'So tell me...what can I do for you, gentlemen?' Straay was careful to appear attentive and commanding. Asking a basic question was the first step in learning something about clients, assessing them. It gave him time to read them, establish something to work from. However, he realised his mistake as soon as silver-hair leant forward. Despite his genial attitude, Straay saw the ruthlessness beneath the facade. Again, he tried to recall where he'd seen these men before. He met those hard eyes in kind.

It didn't go unnoticed.

'Forgive the way in which we have approached things, Doctor, but you misunderstand the formal nature of this interview.'

'Do I?'

'Yes, you do. You see, it's quite simple. I'll start by asking you questions and you'll give me answers. If I like those answers we'll move on, if I don't –'

'Yes?' Straay tried to hide his amusement. 'If you don't, then what?'

'Let's not go into crude details, Doctor,' red-face chimed in.

Straay looked at both men. Silver-hair, watching Straay for signs he was ready to listen, started to speak, but was cut off by a laugh.

'Gentlemen, I'm sorry, but this…this good-spy, bad-spy routine isn't going to work on me. I mean, it's not like I haven't worked for the British Government on occasions. Can we just drop the charade?'

Silver-hair sighed and waved a hand at red-face, who relaxed. 'Well…' He looked a little put out. 'I suppose I like the charade. Fine, we can dispense with the usual tactics.'

'Do they ever work, really?'

'It has been known. I just wanted to see how you would react. You didn't disappoint.'

'I'm so glad.' Straay tilted his head. 'We've met before, I think.'

Silver-hair blinked and then nodded. 'I'm surprised you remember. It was a very long time ago.'

'Twenty years, if memory serves. It's Halloway, isn't it, Major Halloway?'

'Commander.'

If Commander George Halloway was in any way affected by Straay's sudden recall, he showed no outward appearance of it.

But Straay had picked up on something. 'You didn't expect me to remember. Why is that?'

'It's of no consequence, Doctor.'

'Interesting.'

Halloway waited.

'I'm sorry. Please do go on, Commander.'

'You are acquainted, I know, with Colonel Arthur Davidson.'

'I am. We've worked on a number of cases together over the last year. I was about to call him when you stopped me.'

'Well,' he paused, 'I'm glad we saved you the bother of a wasted call.'

'Explain this?' Straay was sharp with his response.

'He's disappeared.' Halloway's reply was unemotional.

Straay stared at him for a moment. 'Disappeared? When?'

'Last contact was made at 5pm, yesterday.'

Mary... Straay thought.

Halloway stood and limped towards a drinks cabinet. Straay joined him. Pouring two generous glasses of whiskey from the decanter, he handed one to Straay.

'It's a difficult case, because we haven't got much to go on.' The commander took a large mouthful.

'What do you have?' Straay sipped at his drink. Red-face continued to watch his every move.

'Before we go into that, tell me, what is your relationship with the colonel?'

Straay smoked his cigarette down to the filter, and then put it out. 'He and I have been friends for a few years. We met on a case in Holland. He was living there at the time, with his wife and daughter. I'm Mary's godfather.'

Halloway nodded. 'Yes, I know. How much contact have you had since his wife was committed?'

Straay looked down. When his thoughts were organised, he raised his eyes. 'Infrequent. When Louise fell ill, there wasn't much that could be done. Arthur and I disagreed on treatment and he moved her back to England. Mary was sent abroad to India. I kept in touch with her, for a time.'

'That was when you started investigating Doctor

Chandrix?'

'No. At least, not right away.' Straay put his drink down and walked towards a window. He sighed. 'Louise is a paranoid schizophrenic, she suffers with auditory hallucinations. Over a period of time her condition worsened. Mary was at risk, as was anyone who was around for the severest of her delusions. Arthur became... disillusioned by the treatment plan.'

'Did he turn to Chandrix for alternatives?'

'I don't know.'

Halloway sipped at his drink. He knew there would be more, so he waited patiently. Straay turned to face him, his expression haunted. He seemed hunched. Older. Halloway understood his sadness. 'You made the decision to break contact?'

Straay was impressed. Halloway's question had been insightful. 'Basic psychology, I like that. Yes. We drifted apart, Commander. You're correct; I lost touch with Arthur through choice. I tried to keep up to date with Louise's condition, though.'

Halloway smiled. 'Thank you for being so candid with me, Doctor; now let me be just as candid. You're lying.'

'About what, specifically?'

Halloway rubbed his chin in amusement.

Red-face said: 'Look, Doctor. You said a moment ago, you'd worked with him on a number of cases over the last year. That's a lie.'

Straay pulled out another cigarette and lit it. 'True.'

'May I ask why?'

'Why I lied? Or why I lied so obviously?'

Halloway chuckled and asked: 'When did you last have direct contact with Colonel Davidson?'

'About six weeks ago.'

'Thank you, and prior to that?'

'I hadn't spoken to him in almost nine years. I had just concluded giving evidence on a case in Germany and there he was, sitting in the back of the court. We had coffee.'

'What did you discuss?' Halloway re-filled his glass.

Straay put a finger to his lip and his somberness lifted. Halloway noted it with interest. 'I've answered a number of questions, as a courtesy to you both. Now it's time for you to answer a few of mine.'

Halloway raised his eyebrows and then acquiesced.

'When you spoke with Arthur, what did he say?'

'Davidson said he'd made contact with Chandrix and we could move ahead with the next stage. He never reported in after that.'

Straay resumed his seat. 'Commander, please explain the situation to me, from the beginning.'

Halloway leant against the cabinet, considering his response.

'We know you and the colonel have been investigating Doctor Chandrix, so tell me something I don't know.'

'Chandrix and I worked together for a while on treatment projects for disorders like schizophrenia. The basic treatment requires prescription of sedatives to suppress a patient's nervous system. About five years ago Chandrix developed some radical ideas. It was clear to me that we weren't going to see eye-to-eye on his research. It was suspect; my peers agreed. His approaches were not scientific. Underdeveloped, amateurish, mediaeval even. But his intelligence is first rate; make no mistake about that. So without funding and support he left to pursue his own ideas.'

'It fits with what we understand about him too. What were his ideas?'

'He believed in a physically invasive therapy, which modern European science has all but dismissed. Hydrotherapy in the form of hot or cold baths for hours at a time; various forms of shock therapy, including using insulin, Metrazol, and electroconvulsive therapy. All of these treatments induce seizures in patients. Chandrix claimed they worked by "shocking" patients out of their illness. He also believed there was a connection between epilepsy and schizophrenia. However, we now know that a patient who had the former, even if it was induced, couldn't have the latter.'

Halloway rubbed at his thigh and then returned to his chair. 'Interesting. It turns out he moved on to blackmail.'

'Arthur said little about it. He wanted me to approach Chandrix but wouldn't tell me anything until I agreed to meet him. I couldn't at the time, because I was working on a case. We met up in London. But the brief he gave me was very thin. So Chandrix did find a way to finance his own research after all?'

'The problem is we can't prove any of it. We know he started using contacts in his profession. Contacts that gave him access to certain medical information about individuals, which was so sensitive, they would rather pay than report the blackmail. He is very careful about whom he picks.' Halloway finished his drink. He left his seat to pour himself another, lifting the decanter to Straay, who shook his head. He continued as he sat.

'We know of a number of people who will still not admit to being blackmailed, even though we have supporting evidence, and they won't prosecute for fear of reprisals. He's clever enough not to purchase compromising letters from servants.'

'There is one thing I can tell you about Chandrix with certainty; he's a specialist at forming connections with specific personality types—he always was.'

Halloway twisted his glass in thought, watching as the liquid threatened to spill out. He shook his head, took another gulp, and sighed. 'We figured that out a little late. At some point he must have changed direction—that's when we became involved. Most of his victims were made to pay financially for their mistakes which is, as I understand it, normal and not a matter for us. But in later cases, the payment became information; information which could and has hurt this country. We don't quite understand how he gets the information, or how he influences people—in some cases it affects high ranking government officials, who are not easy to manipulate. How he gets away with it, is beyond me.'

Straay cut in: 'You just answered your own question,

Commander. He gets away with it because he picks the type of people who shouldn't be coercible; those everyone thinks of as above suspicion.'

'Interesting. Please elaborate, Doctor.'

'I would suggest he discovers underlying faults; cracks in their psychology. Most men, even the most robust and unyielding, have weaknesses somewhere. I daresay you do too, Commander, and it's just a matter of finding them. For some it might be a relationship with a child, for others it could be a wife, a lover, or a criminal activity; even something as simple as revenge. Whatever the reasons, pressure can be applied—at first in subtle ways—and when that person breaks, their psychology is exposed. They may not know it, but by then they are trapped. These people find themselves at Chandrix's mercy. How can they allow this exposure to hinder them? Answer: They can't—but it's not as crude as saying, "I know a secret about you." It's subtle, manoeuvred, and artful—this is Chandrix.' He rubbed his chin as he paused.

'These people aren't treated like common criminals—no— they are indoctrinated into his network—which is the root of his cleverness. These victims have access to the most secret information in the land. Politicians—who aren't always, shall we say the most loyal of men. The trick, then, is he has to know already what their weaknesses are and he also knows they will bow to that type of pressure. Chandrix is no fool, whatever you or others may think. He doesn't risk choosing anyone who won't crack. What does he need with the servants and their masters' indiscretions? This is far beneath him. We can assume he has "profiles" of specific people —from say, post-war Army records, or the Home Office, or from some worm of an official who has sold his soul by supplying information, which led to all of this.' Straay smiled. 'Of course how he was getting this information is irrelevant. The network has grown far beyond him. It's quite ingenious if you think about it.'

Halloway laughed. Red-face looked almost impressed. 'Two years of meticulous operation and planning and you sum it up in a few minutes.'

Straay shrugged: 'It's what I do. Go on, Commander.'

'We worked hard to infiltrate this organisation, and we managed it. We were able to discover a contact in India, and it's there we sprang the trap. It's taken us years, but with the help of Colonel Davidson, we were about to bring it home. We had enough to roll up his entire operation. Now Davidson is missing—and we presume the worst, Doctor, I'm sorry to say. Our entire investigation is hanging on a knife's edge.'

'I see.' Straay was thoughtful.

Red-face said, 'We were rather hoping he might have contacted you. You were with his daughter a little while ago.'

'She isn't aware of anything that can help you, I can assure you.'

'You should know Mary has been taken into custody,' Halloway said as a matter-of-fact.

Straay looked surprised. Halloway held up a hand. 'Don't panic, Doctor, nothing serious, she'll be released soon enough.'

'Why has she been taken into custody?'

Red-face spoke up. 'For her protection, of course.'

Straay thought for a moment. 'Protection from what?'

'From whom, you mean?'

'I suppose that is what I must have meant.'

'What is your next move, Commander?'

'We have one option left.'

'Which is?' Straay already knew the answer.

'To recruit you, Doctor.'

Halloway stood, swallowed the last of his drink, and placed the glass beside the decanter. 'That really is rather good,' he said.

'And if I should refuse?' Straay got to his feet.

Halloway put on his gloves and retrieved his cane.

'Nothing.'

'Nothing?'

'That's right, nothing. It's up to you. We can't force you.'

Straay wasn't convinced. Halloway, however, put an index finger on Straay's chest. 'Just don't forget you still owe us a debt, Doctor. We don't consider it paid.'

'Ah, this again.' He sighed. 'Same routine used on me before—different face this time. As I said the last time you tried to coerce me, it is my father's obligation, Commander, not mine.' Straay kept his response neutral.

'You understand how this works, Doctor, it's not a personal thing, I follow orders. The debt is still owed, and it hasn't been collected.'

'How is this any of my concern? My father's obligations are not inherited, Commander.'

'You think not? For a clever man, your naivety surprises me, Doctor.'

'Whatever you have, you must know it cannot affect me.'

'Hmm, well, if you're sure then there's an end to it.'

'We're finished here?'

Halloway looked into Straay's eye. 'Yes,' he said nodding. 'We're finished here, Doctor. Look, I like you so I want to be frank with you. Your father's obligation, as you put it, this debt, it will follow you—there's nothing I can do about that, but you can.'

'But only if I agree to you…drafting me?'

'Look, all we're asking is that you investigate Chandrix. You already understand him better than some of our best agents, but more important than that, we need to know about Davidson's disappearance. If we can gather evidence, together, we can bring this monster down— a goal I feel we both share. Your knowledge, your special skills, these should be well suited to the task and besides, from what I know about you, you won't refuse a damsel in distress. Mary will need answers. It's in your best interest to help; it serves us all.'

Halloway moved towards the door.

'Can't you remove the monster from the world yourself, Commander? It isn't beyond you, is it?'

'Cut off the head, eh, Doctor?' Halloway flashed him a ruthless look.

'Despite what you might have heard,' red-face addressed both men, 'we're not above the law. We have to do things in a proper legal way, like everyone else.'

Halloway seemed almost disappointed. 'It's a bore, but he's quite right.'

'With the exception of blackmail, of course?'

'Touché, Doctor.'

Straay sighed. 'So if I do this thing you ask, the debt...it is honoured? Finished?'

'Consider the slate wiped clean, Doctor.' Halloway turned his back and went to the door.

'You'll have Mary released to me?'

Red-face grunted a sound of disapproval. Halloway, still with his back turned, said: 'She's rather important to you, Doctor,' adding as he faced him, 'isn't she?'

'Yes, she is.'

Halloway shrugged. 'Consider it done.' He held out a hand. Straay stepped forward and shook it, but there was no warmth between them. 'We'll contact you when we need to, Doctor.'

They left him to his thoughts.

Mayfair, London
The Boroughspade Club: 8:00pm

In a comfortable chair situated in the opulent lounge of his London club suite, Lord Calegray, 1st Baron Dudley and member of the House of Lords, ran a critical eye over the latest political news in the Daily Herald, and waited for his guests to arrive.

He reached for his pocket-watch and noted with mild annoyance that his guests were two minutes late. He slipped the heirloom back into his pinstriped waistcoat pocket and looked up, as a chime reverberated through the expanse of the room. Checking his watch again, he found it was fast. With precision, he corrected it. The arrival of a footman entering alerted him and he folded his paper and placed it onto the table beside him. The servant directed two men wearing hats tilted downwards, concealing their faces, to the Baron.

The first man was dressed with elegance, in a light-grey suit and matching gloves, white pocket-handkerchief, and with spats over black patent leather shoes. At a little over five feet, he was small and, with his barrel-shaped body, had a particular gait. The other wore a shabby, ill-fitting suit of blue that gave the appearance of being a hand-me-down. Unlike his counterpart, he had neither gloves nor any superfluous addition to his clothes. His brown shoes were curiously stained and had mismatched laces. He was taller, a little less than six feet, thin and lanky. They looked at odds standing together; it was clear they were from differing classes.

Together they advanced, accepting his Lordship's invitation to sit. He gave instructions that he and his guests were not, under any circumstances, to be disturbed. Nodding once, the elderly footman retreated and closed the door.

Lord Stanley Calegray was a lean, clean-shaven, handsome man of fifty. As Colonel Stanley Calegray—educated at Marlborough, specialising at the Royal Naval College, Greenwich—he had served with distinction in the Royal Marine Artillery in France and Belgium. It was because of his service in the blood-soaked spring of 1915, where many men fought and died for control of Ypres in western Belgium, that he was mentioned in dispatches and awarded the Distinguished Service Cross.

He unfolded his long frame, walked over to the door and locked it, placing the key in his pocket. Satisfied they would not be disturbed, he opened the drinks cabinet and with military precision, poured three large glasses of brandy, handing one to each of them. He opened up a beautiful, carved ivory box of cigars and put this, together with a large crystal ashtray and the siphon, on the elegant table between them. With lit cigars and plenty of Brandy and soda, conversation flowed into the small hours of the morning.

Brighton
The Royal Albion Hotel: 5th June - 1:00am

Doctor Straay stood on the balcony smoking, his eyes unfocused and his mind awhirl. Under the light of the moon, the sea had no distinct colour. The crests of the tide's ripples shimmered with the ebb and flow. Their beauty had to be seen at night. Straay liked his solitude, his thinking time. It hadn't been a great shock to hear Davidson had disappeared. At some point it would be inevitable. As an undercover agent he knew how to look after himself, and he was also aware of the risks.

Straay winced as the dying cigarette burnt his fingers. His thoughts returned to the present.

Mary, now released into his custody, had at last gone to sleep. He'd prescribed her a sedative, which she had refused to take, settling instead for a number of Pink Gins. They were to travel by train to London later in the day, but he was content to think whilst Mary got the rest she needed. He gave serious thought to how he would approach the issue of Chandrix. It wouldn't be easy because the doctor was a difficult man to deal with: arrogant, complicated. His thoughts then turned to Davidson. His friend. Another difficult, complicated man. Two distinct problems, but both intertwined, connected. Investigating one would lead to the other—but which one should I investigate first?

He continued to stare at the English Channel. It reminded him of his first trip to England, that very first voyage. Almost a man. His father beside him. His brother and mother huddled on the deck of the refugee boat. Memories of his early days brought their share of mental pain; wounds that had eventually scarred over. The nightmares, the guilt, those took longer to dissipate. Some never did.

His eyes moved to the horizon. He saw a vast mountain reaching up from the sea and connecting to the sky above. The mountain, of course, was an illusion—something which, for a fleeting moment and from a certain perspective, resembled

Signal de Botrange in Belgium. In reality, nothing more than towering cumulus clouds along the line of a frontal system. Battling inner demons was part of who he was. He used the word complicated often. It occurred to him he'd never considered that he himself was just as complicated.

Straay turned away from the darkness and slipped into the apartment. He poured himself a large glass of Scotch, sat in the leather chair beside the window and turned off the light.

Mayfair
The Boroughspade Club: 4:55am

Miss Emily Brewster was an attractive young woman of twenty. She was efficient and took her employment at the Boroughspade Club with a seriousness that suggested she was more than just a cleaner. She executed her duties and with practised ease, folded towels and facecloths in neat rows onto her cart before continuing to the next room.

The chambermaid was a stickler for punctuality. She was never late. Neither was she ever early. She believed being early was worse than being late—it was something her mother had taught her and she had never forgotten it. She waited outside the room. She waited, as she always did, for the clock in the foyer to strike. When it reverberated around the complex, she opened the door to the suite occupied by Lord Calegray, and pushed her cart to its customary place. She rearranged the towels for the third time and when she was satisfied, stepped further into the room.

What she saw next, startled her.

She dropped her polish and duster.

And then she screamed.

It was a particular and distinct, blood-curdling scream...

About
Christopher D. Abbott

Christopher is a Reader's Favorite award winning author of crime, fantasy, science-fiction, and horror.

His Sherlock Holmes stories, published in the Watson Chronicles, have been recognized by readers and peers alike as faithfully authentic to the original Conan Doyle.

Described by New York Times Bestseller Michael Jan Friedman as "an up-and-coming fantasy voice", and compared to Roger Zelazny's best work, Abbott's Songs of the Osirian series of works brings a bold re-telling of Ancient Egyptian mythology. Abbott presents a fresh view of deities we know, such as Horus, Osiris, and Anubis. He weaves the godlike magic through musical poetry, giving these wonderfully tragic and deeply flawed "gods" different perspective, all the while increasing their mysteriousness.

Christopher has published with Crazy8Press, and has written for major media outlets, including ScreenRant.

Info@cdanabbott.com
cdanabbott@gmail.com
and find him online at:
www.facebook.com/cdanabbott
www.twitter.com/cdanabbott
www.instagram.com/cdanabbott
and at his website:
cdanabbott.com

Printed in Great Britain
by Amazon

75861780R00109